KT-465-683

Staffordshire Library and Information Service
Please return or renew or by the last date shown

03. OCT 17		
08 FEB 2019		

If not required by other readers, this item may be renewed in person, by post or telephone, online or by email.
To renew, either the book or ticket are required

24 Hour Renewal Line
0845 33 00 740

Staffordshire County Council

3 8014 05114 0793

THE NAKED LAND

Lee E(dwin) Wells was born in Indianapolis, Indiana, the foster son of Robert E. and Nellie Frances Wells. He attended school in Indianapolis and later, in California, studied accounting and became a licensed public accountant and the owner of his own business. With "Pistol Policy" in *Western Aces* (4/41) Wells began publishing Western fiction in the pulp magazine market. As early as "King of Utah" in *The Rio Kid Western* (Winter, 1943), Wells began contributing feature novelettes for Western hero pulps, including feature novelettes for *Range Riders Western*, *The Masked Rider Western* along with more Rio Kid adventures. Authors could take personal credit for these stories as opposed to some hero pulp magazines where writers were forced to work under a house name, such as Wells's Jim Hatfield novelette "Gold for the Dead" in *Texas Rangers* (2/47) as by Jackson Cole. *Tonto Riley* (Rinehart, 1950) was Lee E. Wells first hard cover Western novel. This was followed by such outstanding Rinehart titles as *Spanish Range* (1951) and *Day Of The Outlaw* (1955). The latter was notably filmed as *Day Of The Outlaw* (United Artists, 1959) starring Robert Ryan, Burl Ives, and Tina Louise. Wells learned later in life that his birth name was Richard Poole, and he adopted this as his pseudonym for a number of impressive novels such as *The Peacemaker* (Ballantine, 1954), filmed as *The Peacemaker* (United Artists, 1956), and the outstanding *Danger Valley* (Doubleday, 1968). Whether as Lee E. Wells or Richard Poole, his Western fiction is noted for his wide and vivid assortment of interesting characters and the sense of place and people he could create within his imaginative ranching communities.

THE NAKED LAND

Lee E. Wells

GUNSMOKE

First published in the US by Avon Books

This hardback edition 2012
by AudioGO Ltd
by arrangement with
Golden West Literary Agency

Copyright © 1959 by Lee E. Wells.
Copyright © renewed 1987 by the Estate of Lee E. Wells.
All rights reserved.

ISBN 978 1 445 85068 9

British Library Cataloguing in Publication Data available.

Printed and bound in Great Britain by
MPG Books Group Limited

I

HE APPEARED IN THE DOORWAY with the suddenness of an apparition. Yet there was nothing unsubstantial about him. Though he had not actually entered the dusty office of the livery stable, he seemed to fill the room. This feeling was more than bigness of body, for he was half a head shorter than Will Leahy and hardly half as big around.

Will heaved off the rumpled blankets on the cot in the corner, nerves jangling. There hadn't been a sound and then . . .

The quick flash of a smile broke the harsh angles of the man's dark face. His hat brim shadowed his eyes, but Will caught their amused gleam, like silent laughter.

"You scared hell out of me," Will said. He grinned sheepishly and hitched at his baggy pants.

"Sorry." The man's voice was deep, quiet. "Got a stall for my horse?"

"Sure—sure!" Will walked heavily to the door, and the man stepped aside and out in a smooth, fluid motion.

The lamp above the main doors of the stable threw a circle of yellow light, broken by the dark shape of a powerful, saddled bay. Will jerked a thick thumb toward the door and the stranger led the horse forward. Will studied him covertly, wondering what had given that first impression of size. A stocky body, true—wide shoulders and a chest that hinted of muscles, also true. Will could name a dozen men in Tiempo of the same build, height, everything; yet he thought of them now as smaller than this one.

He lit a lantern within the stable, and the stranger led the bay to the empty stall Will indicated. The man's movements were sure and deft. Lamplight caught the angle of the high cheekbones, the grave mouth, the crooked lips missing harshness by a hair. He saw to the horse first, despite the weary lines on his dark face.

Will led the way back to the office. He named the price, and the man, without comment, reached in his pocket for the coins. Will cut in. "No point in paying now if you're going to stay a while."

"I'll ride out in the morning." The man picked up the saddle roll he had carried into the office. "There's a hotel?"

"Sure—the Palace. Right down the street."

The stranger turned, touching his hat brim with a careless finger. He walked out the door, gone in the same manner in which he had appeared—quietly, suddenly. Will stepped to the door and peered down the dark street. The figure of the stranger appeared in the splash of light through the open door of the Palace Hotel.

Mark Thomas dozed in one of the three cracked leather chairs in the lobby. His head bobbed forward, and the light gleamed from his bald dome. Something stirred deep in Mark's sleep-drugged brain, something alarming. Watery, hazy eyes snapped open.

First he saw the walnut butt of a heavy Colt in a dark leather holster, then legs in dusty dark trousers, slightly but firmly spread. Mark's startled eyes moved upward over a dark shirt covering a muscular chest and then rested on a grim-angled face, the cheeks high-planed, the dark eyes boring deep into his own. The wide lips broke into a smile that altered the stranger's whole appearance, smoothing and softening every angle.

The stranger's voice was deep, quiet. "Do you have some to spare?"

Mark blinked. "What? Spare what?"

"Sleep. I could use it. Do you have a room?"

Mark became aware of the saddle roll at the man's feet and scrambled from the chair.

"Sure." As he moved around the stranger to the counter on the far side of the small lobby, he appraised the man shrewdly. No ordinary puncher or saddle tramp this one. It was something in the man's demeanor, the assured movements, the really good quality of the travel-stained clothing.

"You want the best?" Mark asked.

The stranger came to the counter. "Any difference between it and the worst?"

Mark couldn't help his grin. "Windows on the street. Others give you a view of the trash in the back or the walls of the other buildings. Other than that, no difference."

"Then the best, of course."

As Mark reached for the key on the board behind the counter, the man signed the register. Mark turned it and read, *Hal Graydon—San Antonio*. Mark scrawled the room number and looked up at the stranger.

"San 'Tone . . . a long ways." Graydon only nodded and waited for the key that Mark still held. "Cattle buyer?"

"No." The man looked significantly at the key.

Mark surrendered it. "Be here long?"

"No. Where's my room?"

Mark hastily directed him. Graydon smiled again, picked up his saddle roll and strode to the stairs. Mark listened to the fading sound of his steps. He squinted at the bold, sprawled signature and rubbed his bald pate absently. Maybe the sheriff might like to know. Ray might be at the Long Horn and Mark could edge in a drink along with his civic duties. Jack Zorn was over there—for sure he'd want to know. Mark circled the counter to the door and hurried out.

Upstairs, Graydon found the lamp and lit it. He looked about the room with no real curiosity; he had seen the enameled bed, straight chair and rickety dresser so often before.

He sailed his hat onto the bed, then flexed his muscles. With deft movements of his strong hands, he unbuckled the gunbelt, dropped it on the chair and removed the travel-stained shirt. Then he washed off the grime of the trail. As he vigorously dried himself with a towel already tired with too much use, the flawed wall mirror caught his reflection.

Wiry, black hair clung tightly to a round head with

the ears set flat to the skull. High cheekbones accented the length of the face, as did the straight, high-bridged nose. The sun, deepening a naturally dark color, had made him look Indian. A firm neck stemmed from the powerful shoulders and muscles rippled in the hairy chest as he moved.

He opened the saddle roll and took out a clean but wrinkled shirt. He thought, for a moment, that he might stay the whole of tomorrow in this town, sending his clothes to a laundry before he went on to Arrow B. It paid to look fresh—and feel it—when meeting a man like I. J. Baird, on a matter of so much importance.

Graydon's eyes deepened as his mind touched on a dozen different factors. He was now almost at the end of the long journey from New Mexico, and time was pressing him.

The job in New Mexico would soon be over. He'd come out a little ahead if he could move the men directly over here. Otherwise, he'd have to let his gang scatter or hold them together in idleness, paying them from his own pocket. That could soon eat him up.

He decided to press on first thing in the morning. Maybe he would be suited neither to Baird nor the job. He shrugged into the shirt, thinking it was best to know as much about Baird, Arrow B and the Tiempo country as possible before a deal was made.

Graydon buckled on his gun belt. Tired as he was, he decided to spend some time in the local saloon.

The lobby was empty when Graydon came down. He went out on the porch and stood in the shadows a moment, looking up and down the street. Most of the stores were closed, the buildings dark, only here and there a light. He saw the hitchrack before a saloon across the street, where three or four horses stood hipshot.

As he approached the saloon, he saw the sign, *Long Horn,* and he wondered at the lack of imagination in the cow towns. He pushed through the batwings, moving slowly so his eyes could adjust to the light as he stepped inside.

The room was narrow and long, and the bar faced him, its length running from one end of the room to the other. On either side were two or three tables, one to his left occupied. Two men were standing at the bar, not far from the men at the table. A bartender with slicked-down, thin hair was talking to them.

At the whisper of the batwings they looked around, and Graydon felt their sudden suspicion. He had experienced this many times before, knew that a stranger always had to be weighed and judged in the quick way of the ranges.

Graydon walked to the bar. He caught the eyes of one of the men and nodded slightly. The man looked away, ignoring the polite gesture.

He ordered a drink, then poured from the bottle to the shot glass the bartender spun expertly before him. The bartender reached for the bottle, but Graydon checked him. "I might have another," he said with a smile.

"Suit yourself." The man returned to his friends.

Graydon frowned. He toyed with the drink, waiting for the first low word that would start the idle talk again. It didn't come; the only sound was the restless shuffle of a boot on the sawdust floor.

Graydon threw a covert glance down the bar. The bartender was back in his old position before his friends, but they were not talking now. As soon as they saw Graydon's eyes sweep across them, they looked away.

The place was wrong. Graydon was not wanted here. He felt suspicious ill-will, and he wondered why. Maybe he was mistaken for someone else—no, something more.

He poured a second drink, smacked the cork into the bottle with a finality none of them could mistake. He placed a coin beside the bottle and then leaned against the bar, lifting the glass to catch the color of the whisky against the light.

He heard steps approach across the sawdust and watched the mirror above the row of bottles. One of the men who had been seated at the table came to the bar. His eyes stabbed at Graydon with such dislike that he was startled.

"Dave," the man said. "I'll take a shot."

"Sure, Jack," the bartender answered, and came down to serve him.

Graydon mentally placed the other men in the room.

Two beyond this man, Jack, at the bar—but they would probably move back toward the door. Two more at the table. Five—six, counting the bartender—and all of them acting like fighting cocks toward a strange rooster. Graydon should have left before Jack decided to start things. Might make it even now, and still not look as if he feared trouble.

Graydon lifted the glass and caught the steady, insolent stare of the man at the bar. He was about Graydon's age, but hard work, or worry, had put lines in his face. Gaunt and angular in features, yet handsome in a way, the man had an arrogant assurance.

"A stranger to these parts," he said flatly, a nasal quality to his voice. As Graydon turned to face him, he continued. "Staying long?"

Graydon spoke carelessly. "Riding on tomorrow."

"Where?"

Graydon finished his drink before he answered. "North."

"North—would it be Arrow B?"

Graydon turned to face the man. His eyes flicked beyond him and, as he had expected, there were two men not far from the door and two by the far wall. Dave, the bartender, stood at the end of the counter, his hand below it.

Graydon considered the man before him. The coal black eyes were direct and hard, the thin mouth set in firm, uncompromising lines. Handle with care, Graydon thought, but don't back down. That loses the first trick.

"A man's business is usually his own."

"Anything Arrow B does concerns me and my friends."

"So," Graydon said, "who are you?"

The man checked a desire to look around at his friends. His jaw tightened. "I'm Jack Zorn. I own a spread, like my friends here. A man comes in from San Antonio, heading north, can only be going to Arrow B unless—" Zorn's lips twisted in a sarcastic smile—"unless he's going clean to Dodge. Nothing else north."

He threw a glance at the others, and there was a murmur of assent. A man near the door chuckled—and the sound was not pleasant.

Here was antagonism toward Arrow B, and Graydon knew that it was focused on him by suspicion of association. It would grow stronger if he admitted the ranch was his destination. Though he didn't seem to move, his easy stance disappeared. His hand remained in the natural position, just below his holstered gun, but the muscles tightened in fingers, wrist and arm. Take Zorn first, he thought. Ram a gun in his stomach and the others will be afraid to move. But it will have to be fast.

He spoke, his deep voice slowed to a drawl. "That's right . . . nothing but Dodge up that way. But maybe that's where I'm heading."

"Like hell you—" Zorn started.

The batwings whispered, and every head turned, Graydon's with the rest. He caught the gleam of the star on the black, open vest, got the impression of a stocky man with a square-jawed face.

One of the men by the door blurted, "Uh—howdy, Ray."

The atmosphere of the room changed, no longer brittle with danger. Graydon knew the law, no matter how biased, could not be openly flaunted. He looked again at Zorn. "Nice talk we had. We might have another someday."

He turned, but Zorn checked him. "Now wait a minute. I asked some questions. Who are you?"

The sheriff had not moved from the door, but his hard eyes stabbed about the room. Graydon answered calmly, "Why, for that matter, I'm Hal Graydon from San Antonio. The rest is my own business."

"You're riding to Arrow B," Zorn snapped. "I'm betting you're a gunhand hiring on."

Graydon smiled thinly. "You always put up your money and call before you see a man's hand?"

"By God, I will!"

The sheriff's harsh voice filled the room. "Leave it lay, Jack."

Zorn made an angry gesture toward Graydon. "Anyone selling his gun to those big ranches is our business, Ray. We got a right—"

"I'll handle it," the sheriff said. He came into the room

and stood before Graydon. Graydon judged him to be pressing forty but, for all his thickness of body, there was nothing soft about him. Blunt-fingered hands rested on his hips. His mouth was a thin, harsh line that did nothing to relieve the hard blue eyes, cold and steady. One massive elbow and arm pushed the rancher back.

"Is he right?" he asked flatly of Graydon.

"Not altogether, Sheriff. I am riding to Arrow B, for that matter."

"Look at him!" Zorn said. "He ain't any ordinary chuckline rider. Look at that Colt and—"

"You jump at things too fast," the lawman cut in coldly. He faced Graydon. "You picked the wrong saloon. I'll buy you a drink at the Star. They think more of Arrow B over there."

Graydon shrugged. "Thanks, Sheriff. Only I'll buy."

Zorn moved, but the lawman gave him a cold glance that halted him. The sheriff turned to the door, and Graydon followed. At the batwings, the sheriff looked around at the silent men, then his eyes fastened on Zorn. "Jack, if you want to take over my job, just let me know."

He pushed through the door, Graydon following. They crossed the porch and descended the steps in silence. The sheriff indicated a saloon across the street and down.

"The Star. Association riders hang out there." His voice held an edge. "As you see, the range is split."

Graydon said nothing. A few steps further on, the sheriff asked sharply, "Did Jack name your business?"

"No. I'm not hiring my gun. It's strictly a business deal."

"Jack always makes a bad guess and then rides it to death," the lawman said sardonically.

"Why does he hate Arrow B?"

The sheriff grunted. "It's one of the Association spreads. They're all big and pushy. Arrow B's the worst. Lately there's talk that Arrow B plans to fence its range and that the others will tie in with it. That makes everyone madder."

They had come to the hitchrack before the Star. The lawman stopped, and Graydon swung around in surprise. "How about that drink, Sheriff?"

"No, thanks. That was just talk back there."

"Oh. Well, thanks, Sheriff. . . ?"

"Decker, Ray Decker."

"Thanks for walking in when you did. It was lucky."

"Not entirely. Mark Thomas told me you had signed in at the Palace. I like to know who comes and goes. I looked for you, then figured you'd be at one of the saloons—and you were."

"Sounds like you keep a tight rein on Tiempo."

Decker shrugged. "My job." He indicated the saloon. "There'll be no more trouble—that is, if you don't stay in town. By the way, what is your business at Arrow B?"

"A contract with them . . . concerns their range."

Decker considered Graydon in that level, cold way of his. Finally, he made a resigned motion with one shoulder. "We'll let it go—for now." Then he grinned. "Be careful of that woman. She's pretty enough, but I hear she drives a harder bargain than any man."

Graydon stared. "A woman!" He laughed. "But I won't be dealing with her. I'm to see I. J. Baird."

Decker nodded. "Irene Baird. Watch her. Good night."

He walked away, and Graydon stared after him in mingled surprise and consternation.

II

THE NEXT MORNING, when Graydon walked out on the porch, he found Ray Decker seated on one of the old rocking chairs. The sheriff twisted about to look at him. "Morning."

Graydon halted. "Waiting for me, Sheriff?"

Decker's lips pursed. "Kind of wondered when you're leaving. Thought I'd ask."

"Some people like to eat before they travel."

"Next door." Decker jerked his thumb toward the café and settled back in the chair. Graydon moved across the porch and walked the few yards to the small café.

By daylight, Tiempo looked depressingly like a hundred cow towns Graydon had seen. The wide road looked as though it had rammed through the village, shouldering aside the structures. Because of the street's width, the single horse and buckboard at the far end accented the air of desertion.

Graydon turned into the café. A bell clanged loudly as he entered, and the single customer at the counter looked around. Jack Zorn sat immobile, coffee cup held poised and momentarily forgotten. Graydon closed the door and the bell clanged again. He kept his face expressionless and took the nearest stool.

Zorn lowered the cup slowly to the counter, and Graydon heard the slight scrape as the man gathered his feet under him. Then a scowling giant of man appeared from behind the partition in the rear. Zorn eased back on the stool.

Graydon ordered, and the giant disappeared. Graydon turned his back to Zorn to look out the narrow window. He heard Zorn stand up and walk slowly to the door. Graydon squared around to the counter, his hands folded on the wood before him. He did not move when Zorn's slow steps halted behind him. There was a moment of silence.

"I'm surprised you're still in town this morning, Graydon."

Graydon's brow lifted. "No one told me to leave."

Zorn took a breath. "Ray's more patient than some."

"I've noticed," Graydon said dryly. He added reasonably, "I'm not on Arrow B's payroll and not likely to be. What's your argument with me?"

Zorn eyed Graydon, trying to discern some trick in this new approach. He decided there was one. "You're no working puncher. That shows in your talk, in your hands. They ain't held a rope or a branding iron. Soft, more like they're used to a Colt. It figures Arrow B and the Association is calling in some other kind of man—gunslinger, I'd say."

Graydon started to answer, but Zorn's harsh voice cut in. "None of us like that idea. If Ray didn't tell you last night, I will now. Don't show up in Tiempo again."

He spun on his heel and strode out the door. Graydon held back an impulse to go after him.

The giant appeared, a heavy platter of ham and eggs in his hand. Graydon ate slowly, thinking. This business of his at the Arrow B could involve more than a contract—much more.

There was tension on the Tiempo range. Graydon did not know why, but the area was divided into two opposing camps. Arrow B was a member of some sort of an association of large ranches in the area. Zorn had made it clear enough that the Association was not liked by the smaller outfits.

Idle talk in the Star had given Graydon the hint that the town was sympathetic toward men like Jack Zorn. Graydon had not projected himself into the talk, for he was a stranger, and no one at the Star had struck up a conversation, even though they had been friendly in a distant, polite way.

The contract at the Arrow B could bring tension to a head. It could easily happen, he knew, and he was worried at the thought. He was not afraid of trouble, but no man in his right senses invited it without good reason.

His thoughts jumped to the owner of the Arrow B; Baird—I. J. Baird—Irene. A woman, apparently young and pretty. He didn't know if he wanted to talk business with her. He had never dealt with a woman before.

He finished his plate and sipped thoughtfully at his coffee. Maybe he ought to ride out of Tiempo. But other jobs would not be easy to come by—the whole point. He had been thankful that Baird's letter had reached him toward the end of the job in New Mexico. Now he wasn't sure.

Zorn's warning flashed into his mind, and Graydon's jaw hardened. Damned if he'd run out. He'd ride out to Arrow B and judge the real depth of the trouble before he made up his mind. Then he could move his crew here or disband it, depending upon his decision.

Ray Decker was still sitting on the hotel porch when Graydon returned, and he was there when Graydon came out again, saddle roll on one shoulder. Decker was still watching from the hotel porch as, later, Graydon rode at a slow pace along the street.

Soon Tiempo was behind him, and soon the road narrowed to little more than a trail. There was no sign of man or habitation.

This was rich grazing land where cattle could grow fat. A rancher would want to own all of it he could get. Graydon had an idea that this might be behind the tension he had discovered the night before.

The sun mounted higher. Now and then a trail led off the main road, but lack of signs or sight of house or rider gave him the feeling that he rode through a rich but deserted area. No fences, but he hardly expected any. That would come in due time—and inevitably.

At long last he came to a sign firmly planted where a trail cut off toward the east. Black letters boldly proclaimed *Arrow B,* and a crudely drawn hand pointed due north. Graydon drew rein, his attention caught by the jagged splintering of bullet holes in the sign.

They could have been made by punchers hoorawing on a wild Saturday night ride to town. Or the bullets could have been fired as a symbol of dislike and hatred.

Graydon passed the sign with another speculative glance. A line of low hills lifted some distance ahead, and the road took a turn to angle between them. He kept the horse at a steady pace.

He approached the hills and a shallow pass opened out before him. Suddenly a rider appeared some distance ahead, drew rein and sat motionless. Graydon rode on without hesitation. As he came closer, he saw that there was something challenging in the way the man sat the saddle.

He was tall and slender, and the high-crowned Stetson added to his height. Graydon read muscular power in the set of the shoulders, the lift of the chest. The man's right hand hung loose just below his holster and he carried a rifle in a saddle boot.

"This is Arrow B range," the man said, voice flat with challenge.

Graydon drew rein. "That's where I'm headed."

"Why?"

"Business—my own."
"Might be mine. I'm the foreman, Kurt Yates."
Graydon shook his head. "I'll talk to your boss. That's who sent for me."
Yates' blue eyes widened, and his sun-reddened face broke into a grin. "You must be Hal Graydon. Irene's expecting you. You made it fast."
"I pushed it a little," Graydon acknowledged, and accepted the man's extended hand.
Yates' grip was firm and hard, like the swift, weighing glance that swept over Graydon. "She'll be right glad to see you. I'll ride back to the ranch with you."
"Thanks."
Yates turned his horse, and they headed into the pass. Graydon judged Yates to be perhaps a year or so younger than himself. He had at least an inch or so on Graydon and, maybe, a few pounds.
Beyond the pass, the land sloped down to a sprawling collection of pens, corrals and buildings. It was one of the largest ranches Graydon had ever seen, and he could not help his low whistle of surprise.
Yates grinned. "Some outfit, ain't it?"
"Big enough for three ordinary ranches."
"Bigger. Old Man Baird—he's dead now—kept buying up small spreads or taking 'em over when the owners couldn't cut it . . . and there it is."
Graydon looked back over his shoulder. "How long have I been riding Arrow B range?"
"You come on it about ten miles north of Tiempo. You been riding it ever since."
"And those side roads?"
Yates answered with a touch of distaste, "Little outfits the Old Man didn't buy. Our range goes clean around two of 'em."
Graydon felt a lift of excitement. This promised to be his largest job, and it was coming at just the right time—immediately following a series of small contracts on which he had done little more than break even. He could make money here.
The road made a sweeping curve around the corrals and turned in toward a great, sprawling house with a

deep, cool veranda. The road ended in a branching of paths leading to corrals, bunkhouse, barns and other buildings.

The hitchrack stood several yards from the house, the intervening space smooth and velvety with grass. Graydon dismounted. The house stood strong and proud, two stories of it, with long, narrow windows that stared with glassy arrogance. Gingerbread work covered cornices and eaves, and lightning rods lifted thin metal fingers of admonishment to the sky. It had a proud and slightly forbidding air.

Yates led the way to the foot of the wide porch steps. Graydon followed him, looking from the house to the big, stout barns and the working area of the ranch. Everything gleamed white and neat. Arrow B was prosperous as well as big.

Graydon mounted the five long steps to the porch. Yates stood at the heavy door, broken by a window composed of leaded diamonds of clear glass. The foreman pulled an ornate metal handle beside the door and Graydon heard the muffled, whirring clang of a bell. A fat Mexican woman opened the door.

Yates signaled Graydon to enter and spoke to the woman. "Maria, tell Irene . . ."

A clear voice called from the top of the dark stairs that lifted along one side of the hallway. "I know, Kurt."

Graydon looked at the oak flooring, the ornate wallpaper, the thick closed doors that led to other rooms and tried to imagine how much this house had cost. His head lifted to the stairs.

A woman was descending them with stately grace. She had a tall, slender figure, with full, rounded curves both concealed and enhanced by the high-necked dress. Her shoulders were delicate, yet square as a soldier's, supporting a proudly set head crowned by dark, auburn hair.

Clear, green eyes, friendly and yet weighing, were set in a long, narrow face softened and tanned by the sun. Full lips moved in a smile of greeting, disclosing perfect teeth. "You must be Mr. Graydon. Welcome to Arrow B."

She extended her hand. Her grip was firm, despite

the slender fingers. Graydon found his voice. "Thank you. I'm glad to be here."

She turned to the Mexican woman. "Maria, fix the guest room upstairs."

"I don't intend to stay—" Graydon started.

"Nonsense, Mr. Graydon! Of course you will. That will be all, Maria. Kurt, will you see to his horse?"

"One of the boys can—"

"Please take care of it yourself, Kurt."

Yates' lips flattened. "Yes, ma'am."

He glanced sharply at Graydon and then turned to the door. Irene Baird turned to Hal. "You had a good trip?"

"A long one. Your letter was forwarded to New Mexico, where I was finishing a job."

"Finishing! Then you can start here right away."

"If I like the size of the job and we agree on terms."

"You'll like the size of it. Shall we go to the office?"

She walked toward the rear of the hall and stopped at a door part way down the hall and looked inquiringly back at him. He walked toward her in that silent way of his, and her eyes swept over him, taking in every detail.

He entered a comfortable room, well lit by a pair of tall windows. A desk stood near one, papers placed neatly in its pigeonholes, the working top covered by a brown blotter. A heavy swivel armchair stood before it, and a large, worn black leather chair stood near it. Pictures, furniture, pipe racks, a framed lodge certificate told him that this must have been her father's office and sanctum. Apparently she had not changed it.

A big wardrobe closet of dark wood loomed against one wall, flanked by an iron safe, the door of which bore the legend, *James T. Baird—Arrow B Ranch—Tiempo, Texas.*

Irene Baird closed the door. "You'll find the big chair comfortable. Father always did."

He nodded his thanks and sat down. She took her seat before the desk, facing him. She started without preliminary. "I want my ranch fenced, Mr. Graydon. I'm interested in this new barbed wire and I wrote to the manufacturers. I asked for prices and methods of building the fence."

"So I understand," Graydon said.

"They suggested you, saying that you work closely with them and that you've done some large fence contracts. I wrote to you."

Graydon smiled. "And I'm here."

"Just so," she said, her voice crisp. "Will you take the job? And how much will it cost?"

"I don't know, to both questions, Miss Baird. It depends upon the size of the job and several other things."

"I can show you the size of it immediately. I imagine the 'other things' can be satisfactorily arranged."

She walked to the big wardrobe, opened the door and took out a large rolled paper. She beckoned Graydon to the desk, unrolling the paper.

"This is not a county survey map, but it's accurate enough for our discussion." Her finger traced a section of it. "This is Arrow B—your immediate job."

"Immediate?"

She smiled. "All the members of the Association are interested. Once my fence is built and they see the advantages of it, you'll have jobs from them. But right now we can only discuss Arrow B, of course."

The map showed the town of Tiempo not quite in the center of the paper. Arrow B started just north of it and took up a sizable portion of the map. Within its area, Graydon saw the two small spreads that Yates had mentioned. He read the mileage neatly written along each boundary and suppressed a long whistle.

Irene spoke again. "Slash S and Rafter H adjoin me on either side. They're interested."

Graydon found the ranches on the map. One extended south and west and the other south and east. The combined length of fence for all three ranches was staggering. Arrow B alone was basically the kind of job he liked, one that would keep his crew busy for a long, long time.

"Do I furnish materials?" he asked.

She smiled. "Now why should I pay you a profit for wire and posts that I can buy myself—at your price?"

He grinned in return and studied the map again. He indicated the two small ranches surrounded by her range. "What about them?"

"They don't matter. Will you take the job?"

Graydon thoughtfully rubbed his palm along his jaw. "I admit I like the size of it. I'd have to ride your line. Washes, canyons, draws—even brush—can make problems. They don't show on the map."

"Right now, I only want to know if you're interested."

He pointed to the small ranches. "Your fence would isolate them."

"That's right," she answered indifferently.

"I understand the Texas herds trail near Tiempo. Where?"

Her finger traced a line northward, a mile or so west of Tiempo, directly across Arrow B range. Her fence would cut the trail, forcing the Kansas-bound herds many miles to the east or west of Tiempo. The trail herds meant a lot of business to Tiempo, as they did to every small town along their way. Small ranchers, townsmen and the always touchy trail herders would be antagonized by fence.

"This can lead to trouble—the shooting kind," he said.

She shrugged. "If it does, I'm well able to handle it."

"But—"

"Mr. Graydon." Her voice hardened and her green eyes, a touch scornful, held him. "If you are fearful, please forget it. I'm sure I can find someone else."

Graydon's dark face flushed. "Miss Baird, these things have to be considered!"

Her voice was cool and disparaging. "Please do. Don't be afraid to back off, if that's how you feel."

His flush became more pronounced. "I haven't decided. For one thing, I'd have to ride the line."

"Good!" Her smile flashed again. "You can start in the morning. I'll tell Kurt to have a couple of the boys go along." She went to the door, turned. "Maria will show you your room. We'll eat in about an hour."

Then she was gone. Graydon rapped on the map with a quick, irritable blow of his knuckles. Irene Baird had maneuvered him beautifully.

III

GRAYDON CAME AGAIN to Arrow B through the shallow pass in the hills, but this time two of the spread's punchers were with him, one leading a pack horse. One of the men rolled a cigarette as he looked at the distant ranch.

"It's been a long ride, Hal, but there's the end."

Graydon nodded. Riding the line of the Arrow B had been a long journey. Actually, the job would have few complications. He recalled a rocky gully that would offer a real problem, and off to the west there was a tangled area of sagebrush and small trees that would have to be cleared.

The three of them rode slowly down the slope, and Graydon continued to think over the job. He could make a lot of money on it. His superintendent, Rowdy Johnson, could start the crew and equipment on the way here the moment the last staple had been driven in the last strand of wire in New Mexico.

Arrow B would keep them busy for months; add the other ranches who planned on fencing, and these Tiempo contracts could mean two years' work. And that didn't consider interior fencing for pastures, feed lots, headquarters.

Only one thing made him hold back, the already tangible dislike of Jack Zorn and his kind for the Association spreads. What would happen if barbed wire went up, cutting off town and trail herds?

Trouble—real trouble, the gunsmoke kind. He'd have to figure extra for gunhands or make sure Arrow B and the Association would furnish them. Even so, there would be unexpected delays and losses—destruction of fence already built, theft of materials, secret wrecking of equipment. No amount of gunhands could insure against that.

His thoughtful frown deepened as he rode by the first

pens and headed toward the ranch house. A man was a fool to walk into trouble. But if he turned down this job, who knew when or where he would land the next one?

He roused from his thoughts when the punchers reined in before the house. "We'll take care of the horses, Hal. The boss is probably waiting for you."

"And she's got company," the other man said, indicating two saddled horses at the long rack.

Graydon gave the reins to one of the men and turned toward the big house, working his shoulders to relieve stiff muscles. He crossed the lawn and stepped up on the porch. Just then the ornate door opened and Kurt Yates stood there.

He smiled. "How'd it go?"

"All right. A long ride."

"That's sure! Irene saw you ride in. She wants to see you right away."

He led the way into the hall, indicated an open door immediately to Graydon's left. Graydon took off his hat, brushed his fingers through his hair and entered the room.

It was big and sunny. An oriental rug caught the streaming light in its intricate patterns, and rosewood furniture softly reflected the glow. Ruffled curtains made white halos of the windows.

Two ranchers sat at ease in deep chairs, though they looked out of place in this room, more suited to formal dress than boots, spurs and open vests. A small table between their chairs held a bottle of whisky, and each man had a glass in his hand.

Irene Baird came forward to meet Graydon. She wore a soft gray dress relieved by the gold of a brooch watch pinned to one shoulder. Light from the windows made a reddish halo of her hair and a slender, enticing silhouette of her figure. Her smile was full and warm.

"Mr. Graydon, I'm glad you're back." She held out her hand and Graydon took it. "How was the trip?"

"Good." His dark face softened.

Still holding his hand, she faced the two men. "This is Hal Graydon. He's going to build my fence."

"Now wait—"

She gave Graydon no time to protest but indicated one of the men, who hastily placed his shot glass on the table and pulled himself out of the chair. "This is Bill Spaulding. Owns the Slash S."

Spaulding was a gray-haired man with a beet-red, lined face. There was power in the big body despite the paunch, and his blunt hand had a crushing grip.

Irene turned to the other man. "Obed Hanson. He has the Rafter H."

Hanson was thin as a rail, gaunt in face and body. His skin was sallow, the face all bones and angles, the dark eyes set deep under beetling brows. His jaw was long, the chin pronounced. He smiled, displaying large yellow teeth. "Heard about you, Graydon. Glad you're going to work for Irene."

"I'm not quite sure yet," Graydon disclaimed.

Spaulding's gray eyes pierced at him, then cut to Irene. "I thought it was settled. Something against it?"

Graydon caught Irene's sardonic green eyes watching him. His voice became dogged. "Building the fence is no real problem. I'm thinking of the general situation in Tiempo. Your Association's not liked. You put up barbed wire and you could be up to your neck in trouble—me with you."

Hanson picked up his glass and studied the amber fluid. "Might be. There's always the chance."

"We're willing to face it," Spaulding added.

Irene looked speculatively at Graydon. "But it's apparent Mr. Graydon isn't."

Her cool eyes considered him, and Hanson continued to squint through the whisky glass. Kurt Yates, who had entered the room and stood quietly by the door, grinned widely. Graydon, aware of the flush on his cheeks, spoke stiffly. "Loose words, I think."

"Are they?" Irene asked.

"Let be, girl," Spaulding spoke suddenly. "He's got a say coming."

Graydon threw him a grateful look. "I've done considerable fence building the last five years. Some places take to it easy, some don't. I don't think Tiempo will. If so, someone will get hurt unless there's enough of a gun crew to prevent any attacks. You can't decide a thing like this without giving thought to the consequences."

Spaulding nodded. "Point is, we've already sized up the whole thing."

Irene spoke up. "We're rustled. The calf crop gets shorter every year, and that means mavericker. These greasy sack outfits let their beef graze on our grass. They think anything that grows belongs to them."

Hanson downed his drink with a single quick motion. "With the new outfits springing up, we'll be over-grazed unless we can rope off our range for our own beef. Fence is the only answer. It's a case of a few going under, or all of us. Me, I figure to stay in business."

Spaulding said, "We've had a heap of meetings about this—and it comes down to fence. If you need a gun crew, I guess we can furnish it."

Graydon looked from one to the other, hesitant, but wanting and needing the job. Irene seemed to read a portion of his thoughts. "It's a simple yes or no, Mr. Graydon. If you have any doubts—or fears—then turn it down. We want someone we can depend on."

There it was again, that challenge and that suggestion that he might be afraid. Anger flooded him. Cowardice or fear were not factors, though caution and care were.

The job was big and would make range history. If he completed it successfully, he would be in demand all over the west where fence was to be built. He would be taking a risk—and a girl and three men believed him afraid to tackle it.

"I'll build fence," he said shortly. "We'll work out the terms."

Irene's eyes lighted, and she took an impulsive step toward him. For a split second Graydon thought she was about to kiss him. She caught herself.

"Wonderful!" she breathed.

"Good!" Hanson jumped up and pumped Graydon's hand. Spaulding's massive head nodded in approval.

Three mornings later, Graydon saddled his horse while

Kurt Yates watched. The cinch tight, Graydon straightened and Kurt jerked his thumb toward Tiempo.

"I can send some of the boys with you," he suggested.

"I might get along better without Arrow B around."

Kurt shrugged. "Suit yourself. You'll find the surveyor just beyond the Star Saloon. Theron's store is the post office. Irene's lawyer is above the bank." He grinned. "Anything else I can tell you?"

Graydon chuckled. "Yes. Is your boss always a businesswoman?"

Kurt's eyes grew a trifle cold. "How do you mean?"

Graydon smiled ruefully. "I've had an easier time over a contract with men who thought they were pretty hard. I just wondered."

Kurt smiled. "She's that way, mostly. But there are times when she's human."

Graydon swung into the saddle. He noticed the way the foreman's blue eyes softened as he glanced toward the house, and Graydon wondered, as he rode out, if Kurt had seen Irene in her softer moods. There was a hint that Kurt Yates thought of Irene as more than a boss.

Some hours later, Graydon rode into Tiempo and went directly to the livery stable. Will Leahy appeared and led the horse inside. Graydon considered the street. It was seemingly empty on this warm afternoon, but he felt sure that even now he was watched.

He went first to the hotel and registered, then walked out to the small office of the surveyor next to the Star.

The surveyor, Carl Ames, was a rawhide-tough man in his forties, his leathery cheek lumped with a wad of tobacco. Graydon asked if he could survey the Arrow B boundary line right away.

Ames spat, missing the cuspidor, and looked at Graydon with veiled eyes. "All of it?"

"All of it."

Ames shifted his cud. "Have to get a crew. Ordinarily, I wouldn't want to take a job for Arrow B, but this is too damn' big to turn down. What's it for?"

Graydon's dark eyes stayed level. "Do you want to know?"

Ames thought a moment. "I guess there's no real

point in it. If that woman wants the boundary marked with stakes, that's what she'll get. I can start the job tomorrow."

Graydon left the surveyor's office and walked to the bank building. He climbed the narrow stairs and found the office of Jefferson Trent, Irene's attorney. He explained his business to the rotund, balding little man. Trent leaned back in his chair before a cluttered desk and read the notes Graydon had made about the terms of the contract.

Then he looked sharply at Graydon. "I can draw up a tight contract from these. You won't be able to change your mind about anything once you've signed."

"I don't intend to. Will Miss Baird?"

"Nope." Trent touched the notes. "To review the main points—Irene is to furnish all fencing material and all supplies for your crew, including food for man and beast. You will furnish and pay the crew. You will furnish needed equipment and keep it in repair."

Graydon nodded. "That covers it."

"Method and program of building is yours."

"And Miss Baird can't make any changes in my decisions."

Trent grunted. "Knowing Irene, I wonder how you made her agree to that. And the other clause—that any failure to receive materials or supplies will not cause you to forfeit the contract."

Graydon smiled. "We argued some about that. She's a hard person to convince. But I refused to consider the job without it. It makes no sense to be penalized because of someone's failure."

Trent arose. "I'll draw up the contract. When do you want the paper?"

"In the morning?"

Trent nodded. "You'll have it." He walked with Graydon to the door. "I expected Irene to start this. She's had it in mind for months. I hear she's convinced the Association that every member should fence."

"At least two," Graydon told him.

"It won't be happy news to some. It could be trouble."

Graydon sobered. "There's a chance. We all know it. In that case, what can we expect from the law?"

Trent made a wry grimace. "As little help as possible and all the hindrance. Ray Decker was elected by the small ranchers and townspeople, and they can elect him again. They don't like the Association, and this fence thing will really make them howl. Decker won't help you unless he has to. There's a hundred different ways he could use the law to block you. Figure on it."

Graydon thanked Trent and left. He came out on the street and paused to consider his next step. He decided to go to his hotel room and write a letter to Rowdy.

He angled across the street, his mind busy with the new job. He would start it fairly close to Tiempo so that the town could be used as a source of supply. He would fence west from the road, making no attempt to block it. This would give ample warning to the small outfits that used the road of what would inevitably come.

He was a few feet from the hotel before he became aware that the chairs were occupied by four men who were watching his approach. Jack Zorn smiled tightly when Graydon recognized him. He stood up and moved casually to the head of the steps.

The other three got up, two of them leaning on either side of the door, the third moving to one side near the rail.

Graydon recognized the trap. He threw a covert glance toward the sheriff's office, but no one was in sight. If Decker knew of this, he wasn't showing himself. Graydon's lips thinned.

He came to the foot of the porch steps. Zorn moved a little to one side, black eyes hard and glittering. Graydon mounted the steps and came up on the porch, and Zorn moved to block him.

Graydon stopped. "Waiting to see me?" he asked flatly.

"That's right—me and my friends."

Graydon's eyes cut to the other men, back to Zorn. "Say your piece."

Zorn studied him insolently. "I'll do that. You're back from Arrow B, acting like you've hired on. We don't want gunslingers in Tiempo. We're telling you to leave."

"I didn't hire my guns."

"But you *are* working for Arrow B?"

"That's right."

"Doing what?"

"That's my business."

Zorn nodded. "Have it your way, then. But ride back out of here. Don't show up in town again."

The three men beyond Zorn now stood tense. Graydon's eyes flicked at them, came back to Zorn. "I've got business here. I stay until it's finished."

Zorn glanced toward the two at the door and edged his hand toward his holstered gun. "Your mistake. You're leaving now. We'll see to it."

IV

A FLICK OF THE EYES signaled that Zorn was about to move. Graydon lunged forward as his hand snapped the Colt from the holster. The gun jammed into Zorn's stomach. He sucked in his breath with stunned surprise and fear.

Graydon's deep voice boomed a warning to the other three. "Want me to kill him?"

Their hands froze on their guns, two of them half drawn. Zorn tried to flinch back from the gun in his stomach, but Graydon dogged back the hammer with a deadly click. "The less you move, the healthier you'll be."

Zorn's lips were slack, and he fearfully lowered his eyes to the gun in his stomach.

"Tell your friends to unbuckle their belts and drop them," Graydon ordered. He added quietly, "You'd better hope none of them makes a mistake."

Zorn moistened his lips and spoke without turning his head. "Do what he says. Don't fool around."

The three exchanged glances and then slowly unbuckled their gun belts, let them fall to the floor.

"Now get out of sight. You can get your guns from the sheriff later."

There was a second's pause and sweat beads popped out on Zorn's forehead. Then, the man by the porch rail moved, edging along it to the steps and down. The two by the door made a wide, careful circle around Graydon and Zorn, descended the steps and looked back.

"Out of sight," Graydon snapped. "I mean it."

They marched away down the street toward the Long Horn. Graydon kept his gun in Zorn's stomach for a long, agonizing moment. Finally he stepped back but kept the Colt leveled. "Now shed your belt," he ordred.

Zorn's fingers fumbled hastily at the buckle, and gun and holster dropped with a dull thud.

"Zorn, don't interfere with me again. Next time you might not come off so easy."

Zorn's anger and hatred were blunted by the fear of the gun. Graydon motioned toward the street. "Your friends will be waiting."

Zorn took a deep breath, swung on his heel and marched down the steps toward the Long Horn.

Graydon holstered his gun. His eyes grew bleak as he looped the gun belts over his left arm and looked down the street toward the Long Horn. None of the men were in sight. Graydon thought how strange it was that the incident on the hotel porch had not attracted the inevitable curious. But no one had come out on the street and no one was in sight.

Graydon swung the looped gun belts to his left shoulder and walked toward the sheriff's office, keeping a covert but careful watch on the door of the Long Horn. His right hand was never far from the gun on his hip.

He came to the sheriff's door without incident. He gave the street and buildings a last, sweeping look, feeling the bore of hidden eyes but unable to locate them. He pushed open the door angrily and entered.

Decker was working on a rifle with rod and oiled rag, cleaning the barrel. He looked up when Graydon entered and slowly placed the oily gun on his desk. His cold eyes touched the looped gun belts on Graydon's shoulder. "How many guns do you need?"

Graydon let the guns and belts clatter on the desk.

"These belong to Zorn and three of his friends. They handled them carelessly."

Decker leaned back and studied the tangled pile of leather, cartridges and Colts a moment. "You'd better tell me about it."

Graydon's smile flashed wickedly. "You didn't see it?"

"I've been cleaning rifles, Graydon."

He met Graydon's look, his eyes steady. Graydon walked to a window and looked out. He could see the hotel porch plainly. He looked back over his shoulder at the sheriff, a dark brow lifted.

Decker's eyes shadowed angrily, and his jaw thrust forward. "Don't get any wrong ideas about me."

Graydon approached the desk. Decker looked up, impassive. Either the lawman was telling the truth or he was the finest actor in all Texas. Graydon decided to give him the benefit of the doubt and told him the whole story.

Decker listened. Twice he glanced at the guns. He folded his hands across his open vest, cold eyes level, telling nothing. Graydon finished and waited. The sheriff continued to study him until Graydon's patience broke. "Well, what are you going to do about it?"

"What do you expect me to do?"

Graydon leaned over the desk, supporting his weight on his hands, fingers close to the guns. "Sheriff, I've been threatened, warned to leave town. I took care of this myself, but it can happen again. Aren't there laws against acts like that?"

"There are."

Graydon straightened. "Well!"

Decker lifted his shoulders, dropped them. "Do you have witnesses?"

Graydon exploded. "Witnesses! There were four of them—"

Decker's crooked smile stopped him. "I doubt if they'd help you much. Anyone else?"

"The street was empty. No one was in sight."

Decker glanced toward the distant window. "I didn't see it. No witnesses—just your word against the others. So, I can't see that I can do anything."

Graydon choked down anger, spoke tightly. "You wear a badge. That says you're a lawman."

Decker nodded. "I am." Then he leaned forward, eyes boring into Graydon. "Right to the letter of the law—no more and no less. Someone breaks a law and I see it or can prove it, be damned sure I'll act. Keep that in mind."

"Now what is the meaning of that?" Graydon demanded. "A threat?"

"No—a warning, for your own good and Arrow B's. Something's been in the wind up there a long time. I could feel it. Then you come along. You're not a gunslinger, but it's a business deal and nobody talks. Then you hire a surveyor."

"Get to the point," Graydon snapped.

"Why, man, I'm right there now! I figure you're building fence. That's one hell of a mistake."

"And you—"

Decker's lifted palm checked Graydon. "Irene Baird has a right to run fence if she wants—on her own property. I can't do anything about that. But—" His face grew tight and cold—"I can do plenty if she, or anyone connected with that job, makes a legal mistake. You can depend on it."

Graydon's face had the harsh look of an Indian's. His voice was flat, without intonation. "You're saying you'll do nothing to protect or help me, or Arrow B."

"I'll protect when there's proof protection is needed. I'll arrest when there's proof enough to arrest a man. Unless there is, I won't move. Don't ask me. You can also figure I'll be watching you and Arrow B."

"You make it pretty clear, Decker. I'd better not get a whisker out of line or you'll be on my back. But if something happens to me, you'll manage to look the other way. That's a hell of a way to ramrod the law."

The sheriff spoke patiently. "Don't tell me about the law, and don't figure me for a fool. I know my duties. If you come to me with a complaint backed by real evidence, I'll act. But don't bring in some witness who's on your payroll, or Arrow B's, and who'll lie like hell to stay there."

"Anyone working for me would be a liar?"

"Not necessarily, but I'd have to be damn' sure." Now Decker's voice held a more reasonable note. "I've got no personal argument with you or Arrow B. But neither you nor the Association ranches elected me. The votes came from all the little spreads and the people in this town. They can elect me again."

"So you'll favor them, come hell or high water!"

"But not beyond the law. If one of them commits a crime, I'm after him. But I'd better have seen the crime or know for damn sure he done it. That's the way it is. Neither you nor Arrow B ever will be able to haul me into court on charge of malfeasance in office. Like I said, I'm no fool. Do you have an idea where I stand now?"

Graydon nodded. "I understand you, Decker."

"Make sure you do."

Their eyes locked another long minute, then Graydon wheeled and strode from the office.

Two men were loafing on the porch of the Long Horn now, and, with knowing grins, they watched him walk to the hotel. He went directly to his room, slammed the door, sailed his hat on the bed and strode to the window. Decker had laid it out pretty clear, confirming Trent's opinion. The pudgy lawyer might be kept pretty busy, Graydon thought angrily.

He had a biased lawman breathing down his neck. Hitch a horse at the wrong place, cuss on Sunday, have one drink too many, talk a little too loud and so "disturb the peace"—any of these things would give Decker a chance to act. Graydon could see himself, his foreman, or half his crew in jail. That would really hamstring work on the fence.

A stubborn determination built up under his anger. So they tried to drive him out of town, so they said he couldn't build a fence, so they would throw everything in his way to stop him! His jaw set and his eyes grew bleak. There was a direct challenge here: He could build fence—or he could run.

Movement in the street caught his attention, and he saw Jack Zorn and his three friends disappear into the sheriff's office. Graydon leaned against the edge of the window and waited. The sheriff's door opened and the four men came out. All four now wore their gun belts. That could be expected, Graydon thought. They moved toward the Long Horn, talking among themselves, Zorn dominating the conversation.

Once he looked toward the hotel and said something to a companion, who shook his head and jerked his thumb back toward Decker's office. Then the four moved beyond the frame of the window and out of sight. Graydon remained a moment, fingers beating on the window sill. The way things began to shape up, he wondered if he had charged enough to build Irene Baird's fence.

Some time later, he came out of the hotel and turned toward the General Store, remembering that the town post office was there. He thought that, after he had mailed the letter of instructions to Rowdy, he'd go to the Star, the one place in Tiempo where he might avoid trouble. He passed the Long Horn, ignoring the stares of the loafers on the porch. One of them wheeled and pushed through the batwings. Graydon walked on.

A horse, tied to the store's hitchrack, stood with drooping head between the shafts of a buckboard. A boy in overalls and shapeless hat sat on the wagon seat, chucking pebbles at a distant, empty beer bottle.

The boy stared at Graydon as he walked by, and Graydon judged him to be around ten or twelve. The boy's eyes were pinched, mean and insolent. As Graydon turned into the store, the boy spat into the dust, a deliberate gesture.

Graydon felt a flash of anger, but dismissed it. It was one of those things a naturally mean kid would do to irritate an adult.

He walked down the narrow aisle toward the little cubicle with the barred window that marked the post office. Two men and a woman stared at him with a mixture of curiosity and dislike, an indication that word about him had already circulated. The storekeeper took his time in getting back to the window and Graydon had to hold onto his patience. At last the man accepted the letter, looking suspiciously at the address. Graydon wheeled and walked out.

The mean-eyed kid was standing near the saloon now. He had found a new supply of pebbles and a new target, a tin can across the street. Zorn was standing at the foot of the saloon steps, one of his three friends beside him. The other two were leaning against the porch rail.

They were waiting for Graydon. He could see it in their eyes. Graydon's eyes swung across the street to the sheriff's office.

He was surprised to see Decker leaning against a post, thumbs hooked in his gun belt. He's in on it, Graydon thought, and then rejected it. Decker had plainly stated his position, and Graydon believed him. If Zorn made the first hostile move, Decker would block him. But Graydon himself had to be careful to keep even his shadow in line.

Graydon judged the whole situation in a flash, not breaking his steady stride. He watched Zorn and the men on the porch. The boy turned to stare at him a moment, then stepped off the planked sidewalk into the street. His pinched eyes watched Graydon with insolent, unspoken defiance.

Graydon moved on, still watching the men on the porch. They were waiting for a signal that would come from Zorn, Graydon thought. He watched for the slight flick of eyes or muscle that would signal the beginning of the action.

A small, hard object struck the back of his neck just below the ear. It felt like the jolting sting of a bee. A rock!

Graydon swung around in time to see the boy throw another pebble directly at his head. Graydon ducked and took an angry step toward the boy, who whirled about and ran.

Graydon whipped around again. The two men on the porch had their hands on their holsters, and Zorn and his companion had taken a step toward him. Graydon surprised a gleeful look on Zorn's angular face.

Graydon's swift change of direction stopped them. His dark eyes raked them contemptuously. "You put the kid up to it." The four stood motionless, not answering.

"You'd have jumped me for assaulting the boy—is that it?"

Graydon looked from one motionless man to the other and saw that he was right. His eyes swung to Zorn and his lips curled. "That's worse than hiding behind a skirt. It's a yellow-bellied play."

High color flamed in Zorn's cheeks, and he swayed forward, hand jerking to his holster. His companion grabbed his wrist. "Jack! Don't start nothing! Decker won't—"

Zorn eased back on his heels and the man released his wrist. Graydon waited a long moment, but no one made a move. With a throaty sound of disgust, Graydon strode around Zorn and his friend. He walked on to the hotel, presenting his back to them, deliberately showing his contempt.

But beneath his anger, he wondered what Irene Baird had done in the past to create so much hate for Arrow B.

V

THE NEXT AFTERNOON Graydon returned to the Arrow B. As he entered the house, Irene called to him from the office. She was sitting at the desk when he entered the room. "Did Jeff draw up the contracts?"

He nodded. She held out her hand eagerly for the document. Graydon gave it to her. Her dark bronze hair formed a frame for her face, giving it a new, soft quality. Graydon watched her as she read, struck again by her beauty and wondering how such a lovely girl could stir up so much dislike in Tiempo.

She scanned the pages of the contract, then placed it on the desk. "It seems all right to me. Ready to sign?"

"I'm ready."

They both signed, and Irene placed her copy of the contract in the safe. "How about the surveyor?"

"Ames is at work now," Graydon answered. "I sent

word to my foreman to bring the crew on as soon as they're free in New Mexico."

The old crispness returned to her voice. "What are your plans?"

"I'd like to keep in touch with the surveyors while I wait for my own crew."

"Arrow B will be your headquarters until the work starts," she said. She arose and her smile again warmed her face. "I think we should celebrate tonight. I'll tell Maria to cook something special. Kurt will have supper with us." She extended her hand as though to seal the contract beyond the signatures. "We build a fence, Mr. Graydon."

When Graydon came down from his room that night, Kurt had already come to the house, dressed for the occasion in gray shirt and black trousers tucked into polished boots. His blond hair had been slicked down and combed. He and Irene were standing at a small table against the far wall when Graydon entered the big living room. He saw that Irene had provided whisky for them and wine for herself.

She wore a silver gown with full, flowing skirt and bustle. Graydon saw the gleam of a pendant jewel above the low-cut V of the gown that revealed the shadow of the cleft between her breasts. The delicate red of her cheeks glowed through the thin layer of powder she had applied, and her hair was piled high, with small curls at the ears and along the neck.

Graydon stopped just within the door, his appreciation showing in his eyes. Irene was aware of it, and pleased. A new touch of warmth sounded in her voice. "Good evening, Mr. Graydon. It's so good you could come to our party. I think a toast is in order before Maria serves. What is your pleasure, sir?"

Her sparkling gaiety keyed the whole of the evening. Maria announced the meal and Irene offered her arm to each of the two men. "It's not often a girl can have two such handsome escorts."

The food was, basically, ranch cooking, but Maria had added Spanish sauces and touches, and everything was delicious. Yates took little part in the conversation at the table. Several times Graydon caught his covert look, his eyes glinting with a new born suspicion and uncertainty. Graydon wondered if Kurt Yates was more than foreman here, then dismissed the thought as none of his business.

Back in the main room again, they talked idly for perhaps an hour or more. Then Irene spoke reluctantly. "Well, it's getting late, gentlemen. It's been a lovely evening, and I thank you both."

Yates and Graydon stood up, Yates awkwardly, as though he was not quite certain what to say. Irene smiled at him. "Good night, Kurt."

He hesitated, reluctant to go, then he bobbed his head and strode from the room. In a moment, the outer door closed. Graydon smiled at Irene. "An evening I'll long remember. My thanks."

She sat down again. "Don't go, Mr. Graydon. I seldom see a new face, and it's good to talk to you."

He sat down again and said, "I'm surprised that you don't have company more often."

"Surprised?"

"I'd think many a young man would come this way—unless they are all blind in Tiempo."

Her smile faded slowly, and a strange, hard look came into her eyes. "The ranch seems to take all my time."

He nodded. "Arrow B is big."

"I didn't know how big, really, until Father died."

"Your mother?" he asked gently.

"I hardly knew her. It was always Father. He taught me all I know. He taught me that business is always something apart from people. You don't let feelings enter into it, even your own. If you do, you'll eventually lose."

"A hard credo."

"This is a hard country, Mr. Graydon. My father fought Comanches, outlaws and rustlers. You know what I fight. If Father had shown weakness, Arrow B would not be what it is."

"And if you showed any, it would be destroyed?"

"Exactly. Father knew the value of striking first. So do I."

He began to understand the antagonism toward her.

She saw the slight frown on his dark face. "You don't approve?"

"It's your ranch, Miss Baird."

"Irene, please," she suggested.

He smiled. "I like that. And you know my name. But this other business—you could strike at the wrong place, time and person."

"I suppose so. But then I believe that all people, including myself, should take chances." She walked to the little table. "I'll have some more wine. Anything for you, Mr.—Hal?"

He nodded and she busied herself at the table. Graydon eased back in his chair, studying her. Her father had taught her a stern credo, but he wondered if she completely believed it. Granted she could be cold and impersonal, but still he had noticed that a basic warmth often broke through her hard shell. Graydon had the feeling that she was a woman at war with herself.

His eyes dwelt on her full figure and her lovely face. So men did not come here because of her! Could that be wholly blamed on dislike of Arrow B? He doubted it.

There was something in Irene herself. There was the way in which she had dismissed Kurt Yates, her drive to get the best of a business deal. Irene liked to dominate people. A new idea struck him. At that moment Irene turned, crossed the room and handed him the glass. He sipped the whisky and spoke casually. "Too bad Kurt had to leave."

"He has a long day tomorrow."

Graydon nodded. "Still, I felt he wanted to stay with us a while."

"Undoubtedly," she answered dryly. "Because of you."

"What!"

She smiled ruefully. "Kurt's in love with me. I've been aware of it for some time."

Graydon stared blankly. "But—"

"He thinks you might become a rival."

Graydon found his voice. "I certainly didn't know that you and he—"

"It's Kurt, not me. He's a good foreman, but I'd never consider him as a husband. He's never quite sure of himself, even when he's right. He's never quite worked up the courage to tell me how he feels. I know, of course. Any woman would." She sighed. "I could never love him, but I'd have a better opinion of him if he had the —well, guts—to speak out."

She sipped moodily at her wine. Graydon knew his idea had been right. She was sick of dominating, though she continued it out of long habit. She was waiting for someone to storm her defenses, someone to respect. What would happen then? he wondered. He finished his drink and stood up.

"Both of us face a long day tomorrow."

She placed her glass on the table beside her chair. "I'm afraid so. Good night, Hal."

The days that followed were extremely busy. Most of the time, Graydon was in the saddle. Just as often he spent days at the surveyors' camp as they worked their way westward along the boundary, leaving a trail of stakes behind them. Word came from Rowdy that the New Mexico job was finished, and that the crew and its equipment would soon be on the way.

A week later, just at sundown, a line of wagons came through the pass in the hills. Graydon stepped out of the house, watched for a moment, then turned and called down the hall to the office.

"Here comes my crew."

In a moment, Irene stood beside him, looking toward the approaching cavalcade. "It takes that many to build a fence?"

He laughed. "Cook, hostlers, blacksmiths, post-hole diggers, men to set posts and stretch wire. It takes that many people to build a fence fast and cheap." He watched them a moment. "Where can they camp?"

She indicated a level spot beyond the corrals. "Out there."

After a time, Graydon walked out to meet the first team as the man beside the driver jumped down from the high seat. Graydon waved toward the place Irene had indicated. "Pull in over there," he yelled above the rattle of the wagons. The driver lifted his whip in acknowledgement.

The man who strode toward Graydon was fairly young, with a square-jawed, freckled face broken by a wide grin. Fiery red hair escaped from under his battered hat brim. "Here's the gang, Hal!"

"Rowdy!" Graydon's smile flashed in honest pleasure. He winced slightly at Rowdy's tremendous grip. "You made fast time."

"Traveled straight through." Rowdy's flecked green eyes circled the corrals and buildings. "Damn' near as big as a town. If the rest of the ranch fits this—"

"A big job, Rowdy," Graydon chuckled. "Let's talk to the boys."

The two moved into the milling circle of wagons, horses and men. Coarse voices yelled greetings to Graydon and he spoke or waved in return.

The fencing crew was a motley aggregation—big, heavy-muscled, flat-faced Irishmen who could wield shovel, hammer or post-hole digger all day and still brawl all night; dark, wiry Mexicans whose short, slender forms hid muscles as resilient and strong as rawhide; Indians, expressionless except for an occasional grunt and a flashing smile, moved with the born grace of wilderness men about their tasks; the Chinese cook, whose ivory-yellow face popped up over a wagon bed and whose singsong voice called a cheery greeting.

Kurt Yates sent a wrangler to handle the work horses and drive them to a nearby pasture. Graydon asked Rowdy to keep the men in line and to get acquainted with Yates and the punchers.

"We'll be seeing a lot of them, so make sure the boys get along. I want to talk to Miss Baird about the starting point."

"Miss? A woman?"

Graydon nodded. "Pretty and young, but no nonsense."

"Ain't that a shame!" Rowdy grinned, and Graydon chuckled as he turned away.

In the ranch office, Graydon and Irene considered the general map she had shown him before. She pointed to the place where the road crossed the Arrow B line. "We'll start there," she said flatly. "The first thing is a gate. Then build both ways from it."

Graydon shook his head. "We build in one direction. Otherwise, we split the crew."

She made a little gesture with her hand. "You know best. But the gate will be first."

He made a mental reservation on that and studied the map again. "We'll start at the road."

Irene nodded. "How about the work camp?"

He indicated a spot from which several miles of the proposed fence would be equidistant. "The first one here. We'd better get the material from Tiempo tomorrow, and I'll set the men to building it."

Early the next day, a string of empty wagons rolled into the northern end of Tiempo's main street. Graydon and Kurt rode on either side of Irene, leading the procession. Graydon had permitted his whole fencing crew to come along. As they rolled to the lumber yard, people along the street stopped to stare. Doorways and windows were filled with curious faces. Irene dismounted, and Graydon called Rowdy.

"The Star Saloon." He indicated the place. "Let the boys have fun, but keep an eye on them. No trouble."

Rowdy was the first to the bar. He had a drink and listened to the loud, boisterous talk of the men. It was good to belly up to a bar again after those grueling, dusty miles. He caught his reflection in the bar mirror and saw the dark, red mark of the cut he had given himself while shaving this morning, reminding him he needed a new razor. He'd best get it now before he forgot it.

He pushed through the men and walked out on the porch, then walked over to the general store. He entered and stopped a moment to adjust his eyes to the shadowy interior. Then he moved slowly down an aisle and saw razors on a shelf in a glass case. He leaned against it, looking at the merchandise.

A soft voice spoke close at hand. "Yes, sir?"

He looked up, startled. A girl stood on the other side of the counter. Dark eyes met his and slid away at his bold, surprised gaze. Soft brown hair, pulled back from a high forehead, came to her shoulders. He became aware of the full, rich swell of the breasts, chastely covered by a bright, cotton dress. White ruffles bordered the sleeves that ended just below her elbows, revealing softly tanned arms.

The girl flushed under his stare. "Can I help?"

Rowdy caught his voice. "Who are you?"

Her eyes widened. "Mary Carr. I work here."

His admiring glance swept over her. "Good! Then I'll trade here."

Her lips, full and red, parted in a smile. "We are always glad to have customers. Now, what was it you wanted?"

Rowdy now found reason to be careful and selective. Razor after razor was exhibited, replaced. Finally, he reluctantly chose one.

She wrapped the package and handed it to him. "Do come again, Mr. . . . Mr. . . ?"

"Johnson, ma'am, Rowdy Johnson."

"You're new to Tiempo. Are you working here?"

"For a long time—at Arrow B."

She pushed the package toward him with a curt little gesture. "I see."

He frowned. "Did I say something wrong?"

"Arrow B is not too well liked, Mr. Johnson."

He studied her until the delicate flush again crept into her cheeks. "I'll be back. I don't care what you think about Arrow B. It's just a ranch. But me—I'm a person I hope you'll like."

He turned on his heel and strode down the aisle. Mary Carr's eyes softened and, with a secretive little smile, she rearranged the razors in the showcase.

In the cubicle of the lumber office, Farley Brown beamed at Irene Baird. "Thank you, ma'am. That's the biggest order I've had in some time."

She turned from the counter. "There could be more in the future. Now, if your men will load the wagons?"

"Sure! Right away! I'll call the boys."

Graydon swept his hat from the counter and followed Irene and the lumberman out into the bare, sun-drenched yard. He turned to the open gate that led to the street and stopped short. A dozen men wheeled into the yard, angry purpose showing in every step. Jack Zorn led the group. He flung up his hand, and the men behind him halted. Zorn's eyes stabbed at Irene, at the wagons, at Graydon, and then rested on Brown. "What's this all about, Farley?"

Brown's watery eyes showed a touch of fear. "Just sold some lumber, Jack."

"To Arrow B?" Zorn looked at Irene. "What's it for?"

She lifted her chin. "That's my business."

"Maybe." His eyes narrowed. "Afraid to tell us?"

"Nothing about you frightens me. I'm building fence."

Zorn stared at her and his lips peeled back in a harsh grimace. He took a deep breath, glared at the lumberman. "Don't sell them anything, Farley."

Brown swallowed, his face paling. "But—but . . ."

Graydon's deep voice cut in. "It's already sold—and paid for. It belongs to Arrow B. We aim to haul it out. Do you have any other ideas?"

One of the men tugged at Zorn's sleeve. He bent his head to the man's whisper and gesture toward the Star. Zorn straightened, and his black, glittering eyes impaled Brown. "Farley, don't sell anything more to Arrow B. You won't be told again."

He wheeled and strode to the gate, the men following. Irene stood amazed and speechless with anger, but Graydon spoke quietly. "They've had their say. Now let's get loaded."

Brown mopped his sweating face with a bandanna. "Sure—right away." He cleared his throat and spoke, his eyes avoiding Graydon and Irene. "I guess you'd better buy somewhere else, ma'am."

"You mean you won't sell to us! You're that afraid!"

"I . . ." He squirmed. "I just aim to keep my business, ma'am. Have you ever seen what a fire can do to a place like this?"

"Of all—" she started to blaze.

Graydon's quiet voice checked her. "More trouble, I think."

She turned quickly to see Ray Decker walking toward them. He looked at Graydon. "Is that your bunch in the Star?" he demanded.

"That's right."

"Then get them out of town. They're not to come back."

Graydon's face darkened in anger. "Now wait a minute. They've caused no trouble. You've got no right to order them out."

Decker tapped the star on his vest. "It's a sheriff's duty to act to prevent trouble, and that's exactly what I'm doing. That gang is a threat to the peace."

Irene stepped in front of Graydon. Anger almost erased the loveliness of her eyes and lips. "I'll not stand for this! We'll stay as long as we like and do what we like! I dare—"

"Irene!" Graydon's voice snapped like a whiplash. Her head swiveled to him, eyes big with surprise. "Don't be a fool. We'll get out—for now."

"For good," Decker grunted. "I give you half an hour."

He turned on his heel and walked out through the gate, striding to his office.

Zorn watched the sheriff disappear into his office. His gaunt, uncompromising face turned to the lumber yard, and he spoke thoughtfully. "Build a fence, eh? It's what you could expect of that damn' Association." He looked at the man beside him. "Think we could keep a watch on that crew?"

The man's blank look silently asked why. Zorn smiled tightly. "Maybe we can kill this fence business before it gets started."

VI

GRAYDON HAD PICKED a pleasant spot for the work camp, near a small creek and a wooded area. Already the sound of hammers was constant as the first of the bunkhouses went up. Rowdy stood beside Graydon outside the tent that served as temporary field office. "Won't take long for us to get settled," he said. "When do we start building fence?"

"Wire and posts should be here by the time the camp is finished."

Rowdy grinned. "Maybe we'll have time for another trip to town."

Graydon frowned. "Not a chance."

"Hey, now!" Rowdy faced him. "You know the boys work hard all week and like to play come Saturday and Sunday. It's not easy to hold them down."

"You have to." Graydon saw Rowdy's irritation and his voice softened. "When I see tempers have cooled a little, we'll all ride in and have ourselves a night."

He gave a few final instructions and then mounted his horse. Rowdy watched him ride off, then looked beyond the trees toward distant Tiempo. He had a vivid picture of Mary Carr, the enticing shape of her, the shy brown eyes, the soft sound of her voice. Maybe the superintendent might find a good reason to ride into town.

Graydon rode to Arrow B, his mind busy with immediate plans and problems. He would have to check with Irene to make sure that delivery schedules for the material would cause no delay in the work. He thought of the layout of the work camp and could find nothing wrong. In a few days it would be finished, and then he could leave Arrow B. His absence would certainly make Kurt Yates feel better.

He found Irene in the office and reported on the progress of the work camp. He also told her that he had forbidden Tiempo to his crew. She frowned. "Why?"

"To avoid trouble."

Her eyes flashed. "I think Tiempo should get every bit of trouble that's coming to it. I'm still of a mind to take my crew in there and turn them loose."

"That's the worst thing you could do right now."

"I make up my own mind," she said angrily.

Graydon shrugged it off. "There is something you can do along that line. It's time we find out if Spaulding and Hanson will give us men to guard the camp."

She spoke a bit impatiently. "I'll send riders to ask them over tomorrow."

Late the next morning, Irene made an animated report to Spaulding and Hanson on their progress. She finished and looked expectantly from one to the other.

Hanson nodded. "Sounds mighty fine, Irene. But we heard what happened in town the other day."

"What did you hear?" Graydon asked.

Spaulding moved so suddenly their eyes swung to him. "All of it, I reckon. Decker won't let your crew show up in Tiempo. Jack Zorn has everyone worked up about the fence."

Graydon's smile was faint and twisted. "Wasn't something like this expected?"

Hanson cleared his throat. "Yes, it was. But not this soon. We figured they'd move slow."

"Or take it laying down," Graydon added dryly. "Looks like they won't. So I want the men you promised."

Hanson pulled a moment at his lower lip. "You figure they'll hit your camp?"

"Or the fence."

Hanson's lips screwed up in a grimace. "Man, it'll be impossible to guard miles and miles of fence. Be no end to it, either, so far as time is concerned."

Graydon disagreed. "I want your men for only a month. I want them to show themselves around the camp, out on the job and along the completed fence. If Zorn and his friends have any idea about hitting us right away, the men will discourage them. That will give the cool heads in Tiempo time to make the others see reason. After that, there won't be any gunsmoke."

Spaulding grunted disbelievingly. "What if there is?"

"Only once—if that."

Irene's voice held scathing amazement. "Are you backing down?" She jumped up. "May I remind you that you wanted the fence as well as I? That the Association voted to try it and I agreed to build first?"

Hanson spread his hands. "Sure, but—"

"That you promised to back me, since it was the only way we could see to beat off these hungry graze-grabbers?"

Graydon's quiet voice made her turn to him. "You're tangling your loop, Irene. Neither of these gentlemen has turned you down yet."

Hanson eagerly leaned forward. "That's right, we—"

"Want time to think it over?" Graydon nodded. "But a show of force now will tell Zorn and the rest we mean business."

Spaulding picked up his hat and arose. "Graydon, give us a few days."

"I will not—" Irene flashed, but Graydon placed his hand on her arm, his fingers tightening. She threw him a startled look and subsided.

Graydon faced the two ranchers. "I know you'll back us. Send word when we can expect your men."

"Sure." Hanson nervously turned his hat brim in his fingers. "We'll do what's right."

A few moments later, Irene and Graydon stood on the porch, watching the two ranchers swing into saddle and ride off. Irene stood stiff and angry. She whirled to face Graydon. "Why didn't you let me call them the cowards they are!" she blazed.

Graydon sighed. "They're not cowards. They rushed into fencing without seeing what could happen."

"But they knew! They talked about it!"

"Things have happened too fast for them. I think . . ." His voice trailed off, for he believed that, in her dominating way, Irene had pushed them into hasty action.

"You think?" Irene asked.

"I think they'll back you. But calling them cowards would have made them stubborn."

He saw by her expression that she reluctantly agreed with him. She looked along the road where Hanson and Spaulding were riding toward the distant hills. "I was so certain of them!"

Graydon chuckled mirthlessly. "I had certainty knocked out of me long ago."

The next day, Graydon rode back to the work camp. He turned into the superintendent's shack where Rowdy was verifying the list of staple supplies just sent in from Arrow B. Rowdy looked up at him and said, "Trouble's coming—the camp's being watched."

"What!"

Rowdy pulled his hat further over his eyes. "Let's take a little ride. I'll show you."

Rowdy led the way up the slope of the hills to a small clump of bushes and trees. He circled them, then reined in his horse, Graydon pulling up beside him. Rowdy looked about the ground a second and then pointed. "Tracks. Some of 'em fresh, some old. Just happened up here one day and found 'em. Something else."

He swung out of the saddle and signaled Graydon to dismount. He led the way into the bushes and pointed to a bare patch of ground. Graydon saw the imprint of boot heels, several sets of them. He saw the brown, time-dirtied end of a hand-rolled cigarette.

Rowdy parted the bushes and pointed down the hill. The work camp was in plain sight, and Graydon could watch every bit of activity. Rowdy led the way out of the bushes, picked up the dragging reins of his horse and pushed his hat brim back with his thumb. "I figure there's not much they don't know about us in Tiempo."

Graydon nodded. "There's been more than one man here. Probably spell one another." He looked about thoughtfully. "Get back to the camp, Rowdy."

Rowdy rode off, and Graydon again considered the signs of the hidden watcher. Then he made a wide, slow circuit of the camp, taking a look at each place that might offer concealment.

He found more sign—horse droppings at the base of a low hill where a mount had been ground-hitched. Graydon went to the top of the crest, where a man could lie prone and be unnoticed. Again, the camp was in clear sight.

He rode down to the camp and found Rowdy waiting for him in the small office. When Graydon entered, he asked, "Anything more?"

"Yes." He told Rowdy what he had found, and where.

"There's more'n one?" Rowdy asked.

"They spell each other and watch from different spots."

Rowdy spoke grimly. "We ought to rope one of 'em and find out what it's all about."

Graydon shook his head. "No, we might stir up something before we're ready. Make a circle of the camp every day. But don't act as though you're scouting for something."

"What am I doing?"

"Nothing—if sign shows there's only one or two men. But if you hit the trail of more than that, send someone to Arrow B right away. I'm heading there now myself. I'll be back in a day or two."

Late that afternoon, Graydon told Irene of the discovery of the spy. "They may be just watching," he said as he finished. "Again, they might be planning to hit us hard, even before we get started."

She said angrily, "They're bold enough! I think the spy should be taught a lesson."

"I'd like to. You can help." Graydon sensed that she was pleased that he had come to her.

"How?"

"We've had no word—or men—from Spaulding and Hanson. Send word we need them. Let me have what riders you can spare."

"As soon as I can."

"Remember," Graydon cautioned, "they're not to look for trouble. They're to prevent it. But I also want our friends up in the bushes to see them."

She looked as though she was about to protest. Then she shrugged. "All right. I'll tell the boys you're in charge."

Graydon went with her to the ranch yard. She spoke to Kurt, who looked at Graydon and then went into the maze of corrals and buildings. He returned with six men, and Irene gave them orders. They were to prepare for a long stay at the work camp.

The next morning, after breakfast, Graydon made up his saddle roll and gave it to Kurt to send with some other supplies to the work camp. When he returned to the house, he found Irene waiting for him on the porch. She looked up at him, a touch of shadow in her eyes. "You're leaving?"

He smiled. "I can't stay here and build fence, too."

"I suppose not. But you'll be in from time to time?"

He chuckled. "To ask why you didn't order this, or do that, or see to this. Or to explain to you why I can't build fence any faster."

"Maybe once or twice just to visit?"

Something in her tone made Graydon search her face. A slight flush touched her cheeks, and she moved aimlessly to the porch rail, speaking over her shoulder with a studied lightness. "We shall kill the fatted calf. I promise."

He laughed. "Then I'll come—without invitation."

Someone shouted out in the yard, and his eyes swung toward the sound. One of the hands pointed toward a rider streaking toward the ranch. Graydon hurried into the yard, Irene hastening after him. Men stepped out of the barn, and Kurt Yates appeared from one of the corrals. The rider swept into the ranch area and reined in his horse. His arm made a sweep toward the north as he spoke directly to Irene.

"It's come, ma'am. Whole train of it. Never saw so damn' much wire in all my life—and it's barbed!"

His excitement touched Irene, and she suggested to Graydon that they ride out to meet the train. He smiled tolerantly and agreed, asking Yates to come along to help him check over the shipment. The foreman jumped at the offer.

The three of them rode northward. Near noon, they finally came on the long line of heavily loaded wagons, the drivers sitting in their shade, the big horses standing hipshot in the traces. The wagon boss met them, finishing his coffee.

Yates and Irene looked curiously at the big spools of wire loaded on each wagon while Graydon checked the shipping manifests the wagon boss carried. Satisfied, Graydon, Irene and Kurt rode back to the ranch. From there, Graydon headed for the work camp, wanting to have his crew ready to receive and store the shipment.

When the train arrived the next day, Rowdy's men manhandled wire, posts, nail kegs off the wagons and into the warehouse. The following morning, with an empty clatter, the wagons left.

Graydon told Rowdy to bring his foremen to the camp

office and they would lay out the work. They were in the midst of the conference when Irene rode up and swept into the little office, eager and smiling.

"Do we start today?" she asked.

Graydon laughed. "Right away." He looked around at the men. "Start building fence, boys. We've got it lined out."

They filed from the shack, and in a moment there came the sounds of purposeful activity.

Irene watched from the open door, her face alight. Then she turned to Graydon. "Where are you starting?"

"At the main road, working west."

Her smile held a touch of acid. "A fence across the road will show our 'friends' we mean business."

"I don't plan to block the road yet. That will come later."

She looked at him in surprise, a hard glint in her eyes. "But that's the first thing I want done!"

"Irene, people use that road. We can't cut them off without warning. It's unfair. There's enough hard feeling as it is. Blocking the road now—"

She cut in. "You know what I want." Her chin came up. "That's an order."

"Read your contract again, Irene. You can't give orders. I use my own judgment."

She drew up, breathing angrily, and spoke tightly. "You can stop all work right now!"

Graydon's brow lifted. "Careful, Irene. If I pull out on that order, you owe me for every foot of fence called for in the contract."

She glared, lips parting and then clamping shut. She flung around and stormed out of the shack. Graydon stood in the doorway, watching her set spurs to her horse and race out of camp. Rowdy walked toward him, indicating the racing horse and rider. "What happened to her?"

"She lost an argument. She'll get over it."

Rowdy shook his head. "I guess so. But it's starting off on the wrong foot, ain't it?"

"Why? She has to know that we build fence, not her.

If I jump at her first order, she'll figure I'll jump at all the rest. Now she knows better."

Rowdy shrugged and fell in step with Graydon as they walked to the warehouse. There was bustle and activity everywhere, that indefinable eagerness that Graydon always noted at the beginning of a new job.

He turned to the corral to get his horse and ride out to the job. He was nearly at the corral when Kurt Yates appeared, reined in and swung out of saddle.

When Yates faced him, Graydon realized the foreman was barely holding a roiling anger in check.

"I just talked to Irene," he said icily. "Caught her as she was riding out."

Graydon nodded, no more. Kurt's lips flattened. His eyes swung about the busy camp, centered on Graydon again. "She told you to stop work."

Graydon answered, voice reasonable. "She had no right. Under the contract—"

"This is Arrow B range, and she's the boss. When she gives an order, you do it. No one bucks her."

"In this case, I intend to," Graydon snapped.

"Do you?" Yates asked, almost in a whisper. "I'll make you do exactly as she says."

VII

GRAYDON LOOKED AT THE MAN in amazement. Yates grew angrier, and his right hand moved slightly toward his holster.

"Stop the work, Graydon. I mean it."

Suddenly Graydon saw that Yates was far more in love with Irene than he had even guessed. He had to move carefully. He wanted no fight with Yates, and yet his control of his own men would vanish if he bowed to this threat. Irene was angry now, but she would come to her senses, given time to cool off. Yet here Kurt Yates stood, offering fight as an alternative to blind obedience to the girl he loved.

"Kurt, does Irene know what you're doing?"

"She knows I back her in everything."

"But this?" Graydon took half a step forward, and Yates stiffened. "Irene signed a contract, Kurt. She agreed not to give orders."

"Don't talk contracts, Graydon. She wants the work stopped. That's enough for me."

Graydon wondered if he could get close enough to rush Yates. He spread his hands in a conciliatory gesture and took another step toward Yates.

"Kurt, you don't understand—" Another step. "Irene knows I have to boss my own crew and work. She can't, and—"

Yates snapped, "I'm running out of patience. Do what she says, damn you!"

Graydon read the intent in Yates' eyes. At any second, the showdown would come. Then there was the sudden sound of drumming hoofs, and both men turned. Irene Baird rode toward them and reined in, the horse tossing its head at the harsh pull of the bit.

She read the situation at a glance, and fear touched her eyes despite the imperiousness of her voice. "Kurt, what are you doing?"

His eyes glittered. "I figure it's time he learned to take orders."

"Who told you to meddle?" she demanded.

Kurt jerked as though she had struck him. "What!"

"This is none of your business. You tend to the ranch and I'll tend to the fence—and Mr. Graydon. Is that understood?"

His face flamed. Then he licked his lips and took a deep breath. "You gave him an order. He wouldn't do anything about it. Always before, I've handled things like this."

She leaned out from the saddle. "Mr. Graydon is not a ranch hand, Kurt. You will remember that."

His mouth opened, but she had swung her attention to Graydon, her voice clipped and cold. "You are right about the contract. Build fence as you see fit." Her eyes sparked. "I don't often apologize, Mr. Graydon."

He spoke gravely. "I know—and you aren't now. We both understand the contract a little better."

Her anger started to slip away, but she caught herself and lifted her chin. "Perhaps. I'll see you later, sir. Kurt, ride with me."

With a swift, stabbing look at Graydon, Yates stepped to his horse, grabbed up the reins and mounted. Irene wheeled her animal about and set the spurs. Yates cursed under his breath and raced after her, leaving Graydon standing in a cloud of dust.

He was the victor, but he was sure he would pay for it. Yates had thrown a final look over his shoulder that Graydon could not forget.

Yates had to use the spurs again before he caught up with Irene. She showed no sign of lessening her speed. For a time the headlong pace prevented any talk. At last she pulled the horse in and eased back in the saddle, allowing the animal to blow.

Kurt studied her. "What happened to your mad?"

She dismissed it with a careless gesture. "I'm over it." She acted as though this ended it.

"He had no right—"

"He had every right. He wouldn't let me forget it, either." She lifted the reins and looked toward the far horizon. Something in her expression puzzled Kurt. "I admire him for standing up to me."

"Your Dad wouldn't have taken a word from him," Kurt snapped.

She laughed. "I'm not Father."

She started the horse at an easy gait. Kurt drew up beside her and saw that she was still bemused and withdrawn.

Suddenly she looked around at him, surprise in her eyes at a new thought. "Kurt, do you realize there's no one in Tiempo like Hal Graydon? I've never seen his like before." She continued, not even seeing him. "I wish there had been. Things might have been different."

His jaw snapped shut, and he stared. But she was completely unaware of his scrutiny. Kurt's eyes narrowed as he tried to get her real meaning. They both rode in silence, each deep in thought. Kurt's were disturbing and unpleasant.

In two days' time, routine was established at the camp and the work went smoothly. The survey stakes marched westward, from the road to the horizon and beyond. At the junction of the line with the road, men were starting to dig holes to set the posts. Each hole was just within the Arrow B range so that there could never be a question.

Far ahead, another crew was clearing away brush and grass along the line of the stakes. Others were cutting down small saplings and trees along the fence line. Heavy posts were placed beside each hole, and spools of wire were spotted, ready for the use of the crew. Before the sun had gone down on the first day, posts were set up and the first strands of barbed wire nailed firmly to them.

Graydon looked on the small stretch of fence with satisfaction. It marked a boundary, a definite statement of ownership, the ending of one man's rights, the beginning of another's. This would no longer be a naked land, an uncharted sea of grass and hills and sky. Fence, Graydon thought—the final sign of law and order.

On the fourth day, Graydon checked with Rowdy, satisfied now that the actual work on the line would run smoothly. Rowdy had but two problems. He pointed to the wagons loading at the warehouse.

"I hope Miss Baird keeps the material coming steady. Better make sure. This fence can go faster than we think."

Graydon promised. Then Rowdy asked when the boys could go into town, but Graydon had no answer that Rowdy felt the men would accept. "You can't hold them here for long," he warned.

Graydon pointed to one of the armed Arrow B men. "Can't be helped. I don't want to run a chance until we know how the neighbors will take the fence."

"I could ride in and find out," Rowdy suggested.

"Not yet," Graydon said flatly.

In the afternoon, Graydon rode into Arrow B. Yates

halted by the corral gate when he saw Graydon ride up. Graydon called to him and swung out of saddle.

Yates was withdrawn, although there was no open hostility. "I'm sorry about the other day, Kurt."

"Sure," Yates replied, voice flat.

"Then there's no hard feelings?"

"None. I understand."

He turned on his heel before Graydon could extend his hand. Graydon watched him go, frowning, puzzled by the strange quality in the man's voice. He wondered if Irene was also angry about the quarrel.

As he approached the house, Irene appeared on the porch. She was dressed for riding in boots, skirt and blouse that made her slim and desirable. She stopped in surprise at sight of Graydon. She smiled, her face lighting.

"Hal! I didn't expect you!"

There was no hint of anger in her eyes, in the warmth of her voice. He remembered her half threat at the camp, but apparently she had completely forgotten it.

"Fence problems," he said with a smile.

"Something wrong?"

"We're going to have to get materials faster than we planned. I thought I'd talk to you about it."

She led the way into the big main room rather than the office, as though she wanted to assure him this would not be all cold business. She offered him a drink and Graydon accepted, then brought the talk to the problem at hand. She instantly became the businesswoman, but not once did the warmth leave her voice.

She was excited at the progress and swiftly calculated a new schedule of materials, promising letters would go out right away. The only flash of the old anger came when Graydon said that he was keeping his men from town.

"That's wrong, Hal. You're telling them that you're afraid of them. Let your men go."

"You might be right. I'll consider it."

He refused another drink, saying he had to leave. She sighed in defeat. "Well, if you must!" she stood up, eager again. "I'll go part way with you. I planned to ride anyhow."

"I'd like that," he said.

His saddled horse was still waiting before the corral, and Irene hurried off to get her own horse. Graydon, leaning idly against the corral post, still felt surprise at the change in her. She had always been beautiful and breath-taking, but had been marred by her desire to have her own way, to give orders, to dominate. He recalled the crisp way in which she had talked as though to cut off all argument.

But *this* afternoon! The curt tone was gone, and her smile had been more than mechanical. There had been warmth to her, a friendliness, as though she was another person. This new Irene Baird was someone he could like very much. But did he dare?

She rode up then, and he mounted and swung in beside her. She gave him a wide, warm smile, and they rode off together, heading out toward the distant camp.

Kurt Yates came to the door of the barn and watched them ride off. He stared after them, a muscle working in his cheek. He hurried toward another corral and quickly roped a horse.

In a few moments he rode to the edge of the ranch yard and drew rein. Far ahead, Graydon and Irene were cantering toward the notch in the hills. Yates' eyes moved along the horizon. He neck-reined his horse to the right as he touched it with his spurs. He would make a wide swing and eventually cut their trail.

Beyond the pass, Graydon left the road at a tangent that would lead him directly to the work camp. Irene paced her horse beside him, now and then speaking of the fence or the ranch. They came to a cluster of cottonwoods, and Irene looked at the trees, her eyes alight. "The shade looks inviting. Shall we rest a while?"

They dismounted and ground-tied the horses. Irene led the way to the foot of one of the trees and sat down, removing her hat and shaking her bronze hair free. Graydon sat down a few feet from her.

Irene finally broke the silence. "I know very little about you."

He grinned. "There's little to know. I build fences."

She pouted. "There must be a great deal more."

"There's not much. I was born here in Texas—my father fought Santa Anna. I had three years of war in Virginia. When I came back, Dad had died and I had the ranch. I drove our beef to Wichita and heard about this new barbed wire business. I figured I could make more at it than in ranching."

She laughed. "I thought punchers never quit."

"I'm still ranching, in a way. Anyhow, I went East and talked to the manufacturers. I had money from the beef, and I put the ranch up for sale. I bought equipment, and the factory sent me out building fences, using their wire. I've been doing that for three years now. None of my jobs were very big until this one came along."

She looked thoughtfully out beyond the shade of the trees into the bright sunlight. "It is big, isn't it?"

He said nothing, and a moment later she continued: "But this is big country—and I've inherited one of the biggest ranches."

"You're lucky."

"Am I? It's a lonely business, Hal. It's not for a woman—not what she really wants. Sometimes I wish I could be—well, just Irene Baird, not owner of the Arrow B. I'll bless the day that happens."

"Maybe the man will come along."

"You think so?" She suddenly got to her feet. "I have to get back now."

He walked with her to her horse, then held out his hand to assist her to mount. They stood close, and her eyes lifted to his, deepening and softening. Her lips parted, and Graydon's fingers tightened on her arm. She swayed toward him, and suddenly his lips were on hers. She half lifted her arms, dropped them. Then she broke free and stepped back.

He looked at her, dark face solemn, eyes searching. For a second she was touched with wonder. Then that vanished, and confusion, mixed with an inexplicable anger, swept over her.

She vaulted into the saddle and raked the spurs. The horse lunged out of the grove. Graydon jumped back to avoid being bowled over, then caught his balance. Irene streaked away, riding recklessly.

Graydon stood unmoving, confused. He wondered why he had kissed her. He knew that at first she had wanted him to, for her lips had responded. Then something had happened, and the Irene Baird he had first known had flashed through again.

What had changed her? Graydon told himself he didn't want to know. He was here to build fence and that was all. He turned to his horse.

For a time the area about the trees was undisturbed. Then, from the crest of a low hill, a man arose, holding a pair of field glasses. He stood but a moment, then plunged down the far side of the hill where a saddled horse was waiting patiently.

With fumbling fingers, Kurt Yates replaced the glasses in the case hanging from the saddlehorn. His face dark with jealousy, he jumped into the saddle and spurred the horse around the hill. He drew rein, scowling in the direction Graydon had taken. He sat poised, uncertain.

Then, with a deep-throated growl, he savagely neck-reined the horse and rode swiftly toward the Arrow B.

VIII

IN THE DAYS that followed, Graydon had little time to think about Irene Baird. The work went smoothly, and he had no more than the usual routine problems. But every now and then new sign would show that the camp was being watched.

Once Graydon happened to look up in time to catch a glint of light from a distant clump of bushes. He recognized it instantly, a flash from a pair of field glasses. He made a wide circuit and then moved in toward the bushes, hoping the spy's attention was still held on the workmen.

A horse and rider suddenly burst from the bushes and streaked away. Graydon could not identify the man; the distance was too great and the rider was crouched too low over the horse's neck. Graydon realized that he could not hope to catch up.

Graydon moved out of the bushes and rode toward the fence. He wondered when Jack Zorn and his friends would make a move. He had the feeling it might come soon.

He said as much to Irene and Spaulding, when the rancher visited the fence with the girl. Irene listened, color mounting in her cheeks. She spoke to Kurt Yates, who was sitting his horse just beyond her. "What's wrong with your men?"

Graydon cut in smoothly. "There's nothing wrong. They're good men, and they do what they can." He looked at Spaulding. "There's just not enough. We need more."

"You promised help," Irene said.

Spaulding looked troubled. "Hard to spare anyone right now."

Graydon said, "Irene has managed to send six." He folded his hands on the saddlehorn and, with a move of his head, indicated the fence. "You promised to back her. So she went ahead. I don't think you can afford to renege on your promise. If Zorn knocks the fence out, all the rest of you will have him on your backs. He'll know it, and you'll know it. You figure out what's best."

Spaulding grunted. "I'll do what I can."

"That was promised once before," she said quietly. "What's it worth?"

Spaulding flushed. "Worth exactly what I say. I'll send over those I can spare—as soon as I get back to the spread."

Irene looked at Graydon with an expression that said this was a small gain, at least. Graydon smiled faintly and then called Spaulding's attention to the way the work was divided among the sections of his crew. There was nothing more said until Irene and the rancher were ready to leave.

Spaulding extended his hand to Graydon. "I'm glad to see the way you're handling this. I'll tell the others about it. Oh, and you can depend upon some Slash S boys."

The next day, as Graydon left the cookshack right after the noon meal, he saw half a dozen riders coming from the direction of the main road. At first Graydon thought they must be the new guards Spaulding had sent out. Then he recognized four of the Arrow B men and saw that only two were newcomers. His hopes dropped as he waited for the cavalcade to come up.

They drew rein before him, and one of the guards indicated the two with his thumb. "They're right anxious to see you, so we brought 'em in. This'n—" He indicated the older man—"is Ned Carr. Owns the C-Bar north of the home ranch."

That would be one of the small spreads surrounded by Arrow B, Graydon thought. Carr was a small man, once powerful, but now age had put deep folds in his leathery face and had made him gnarled and wiry.

The Arrow B man indicated the second. "This is Jobe Taylor. He's got one of the greasysack—"

"It's a ranch!" Taylor flared. "Don't forget it!"

Taylor was a pinch-eyed man with a black stubble that made his lips look sickly red and moist. His nose was a bony, ridged knife that gave him the look of a sly hawk.

Just then Rowdy walked up, and there were suspicious looks as he joined the group. Graydon introduced him. Carr nodded, and Rowdy shot him a surprised, searching glance when he heard his name. Jobe Taylor grunted and spat to one side.

Graydon faced the two men. "How can I help you?"

"Help us!" Taylor exploded. "Why, damn it—"

Carr checked him. "A minute, Jobe." He looked at Graydon. "Are you fencing across the road?"

"Why don't we go to the camp and talk about it?" Graydon suggested. "The cook still has hot chow on, or you can have drinks, if you like."

"Don't skitter around the post!" Taylor spat. "Is Arrow B going to block that road? That's a plain question, and we want a plain answer."

"The road is on Arrow B range. I'm certain you can make a fair deal with Miss Baird for access to your ranches."

Taylor's fist smacked on the saddlehorn. "It's what I

thought! The only deal that uppity wench will make is a freeze-out!"

"You're wrong there, Mr. Taylor."

"Damned if I am! You aim to fence right across that road with no chance to get in or out. Then we can sell, or sit there and starve. By God, I won't have it!"

His hand stabbed to his gun, and the Colt whipped up and leveled. Graydon threw himself to one side as the gun thundered, and the bullet whipped by his shoulder.

Carr sank his spurs in his horse and hurled himself at Taylor. Jobe's gun was cocked for a second shot, but the impact of the horses made the bullet go wild. Carr grabbed the gun and held on, though Taylor tried to wrench it free.

Graydon lunged to help, and Rowdy sprang toward the struggling men. Taylor swung wild blows at the older man as he tried to free the weapon. Graydon grabbed his leg, and Taylor tried to kick him off. The horses pranced and skittered, kicking up dust, their hoofs threatening injury to Graydon and Rowdy. The Arrow B men moved in, one of them throwing his arms around Taylor, pinioning the man in squirming helplessness. Carr twisted brutally, and Taylor's fingers opened spasmodically.

Carr jerked back, holding Taylor's gun by the muzzle. One of the Arrow B men lifted his gun to bring the barrel down on Taylor's head. Graydon's muscles bunched as his fingers gripped Taylor's belt, and he pulled him bodily from the saddle.

Rowdy stepped in and helped Graydon jerk Taylor to his feet. Rowdy spoke through set teeth. "I think this jasper has a lesson coming."

"Let be," Graydon panted. "No real harm done."

"Hal, he tried—"

"We let him go." Graydon suddenly shoved Taylor away. He drew his gun and leveled it at the man's stomach. "Now get out of here."

"Do as he says, Jobe," Carr admonished.

Taylor looked up at his companion, and his moist lips twisted. "Damn you! I could've killed him! I'll not forget the way you turned on me."

Graydon cut in. "Listen to your friend, Taylor. Mount up."

Taylor glared, then grabbed his horse's reins. He swung into saddle, wheeling his horse about and racing off the way he had come.

Graydon holstered his gun and looked at Carr. "I owe you thanks."

"You owe me nothing," Carr said shortly. "I don't like this fence any more'n Jobe. I'll not stand by while you cut me off. But I don't like to see a man killed in hot anger. Jobe was wrong there."

Graydon nodded. "I tried to tell him arrangements could be made about the road."

Carr's leathery face mirrored disbelief. "Yes, you did. But Jobe don't believe it, knowing Arrow B."

"And you?"

Carr shoved Taylor's gun in his waistband and lifted the reins. "Why, I know what Jobe does. You will hear from me and my friends. You can depend on it."

He swung the horse around and rode off. Graydon's lips flattened for a second, and then he turned to the Arrow B guards. "I guess that's warning enough."

"We'll keep close watch for sign."

"You do that," Graydon said dryly and walked away.

Rowdy caught up with him. "This Carr gent. Where's his ranch?"

"In the middle of Arrow B. The map will show you—the C-Bar."

"I hope we have no trouble with him," Rowdy said.

Graydon looked at him in surprise. "First time I ever knew you wanted to ride around trouble."

He walked off. Rowdy thought, Ned Carr—has to be Mary's father. A hell of a thing.

The following Saturday morning, Graydon headed for the road, knowing that the Arrow B crew would be riding to Tiempo. He wanted to pick up the last of the detailed maps from the surveyor and order some minor items for himself and the camp. He would invite less trouble going in with the ranch crew than he would alone.

The Arrow B riders, headed by Kurt Yates, were surprised to see him, and Graydon instantly noticed the increased coldness in the foreman. Graydon swung in with the crew when Yates indifferently made him welcome.

They rode into Tiempo, and once again Graydon saw the harsh looks thrown at them, but there was no open hostility. In the Star Saloon, Graydon had a drink and then told Yates he would come back later and join them in another.

"Sure," Yates grunted.

Graydon went first to the General Store. The few customers glowered at him, and the pretty girl who waited on him was distantly polite. He made his purchases and then went out on the street again.

As he walked to the surveyor's office, five riders, Jack Zorn among them, turned in at the Long Horn. Zorn remained in the saddle as his companions dismounted, his black eyes following Graydon along the far walk. He glanced toward the jail.

He called to his friends, "I wonder where Ray could be."

Their eyes cut to the sheriff's office, then back to him. Zorn rolled his tongue inside his cheek. "There's two ways of doing a thing. Like that Arrow B fence—we could tear it down, or . . ."

He turned to stare directly at the surveyor's office. Then he looked down at his friends. They exchanged quick glances, and one of them hitched at his gun belt.

"How you figure it, Jack?"

Zorn swung out of saddle.

In the small office, Graydon examined the last of the detailed section maps. Ames watched him, heavy lidded, and grunted at Graydon's compliment.

"Just pay for it," Ames said in self-disdain. "Running line for a damn' fence! It'll take a long time for me to live that down."

Graydon rolled the maps. "There'll be a lot of fence in this country—big and small ranches alike. You'll see."

"Not the way I hear it. You'll be lucky if you finish this one."

Graydon turned to the door, spoke over his shoulder.

"Mark what I say. You'll run lots of fence line—for everybody."

He stepped out onto the walk, his attention on Ames back in the office. He sensed someone near him, and his nerves jangled an alarm. A gun bored into his back.

"Easy, fence-man! Easy!" A voice growled.

His gun was lifted from the holster. Now men were crowding close, and Jack Zorn was smiling at him without mirth. "We'll have a talk, Graydon."

He turned on his heel and marched around the corner of the office. "Walk, fence-man," ordered the man who was holding the gun in Graydon's back, and the muzzle bored deeper.

Men were now standing at Graydon's left and right. One of them jerked his thumb toward the corner of the building, his face grim. Graydon, every muscle tensed, walked down the wide passage between the office and the tall building next to it. In the rear was an area of packed, hard earth, the livery stable corral and windowless backs of buildings hemming it in on every side.

Zorn waited for the little procession. Graydon walked up to him, his dark face set, eyes level and hard.

"Say your piece, Zorn."

"Ain't there something about actions being better'n words?" Zorn asked softly.

Without warning, his fist exploded in Graydon's face.

IX

GRAYDON FELL BACK into the arms of one of the men behind him. Before he could catch his balance, he was shoved toward Zorn, who raised his knee. Graydon managed to twist slightly so the blow did not come directly into his groin, but the force of it doubled him up. Then a boot smashed into his side.

Blinded with pain and gasping for breath, he pulled his head down in an instinctive effort to fend off the blows.

He saw Zorn's legs before him and lunged forward, head lowered.

He struck Zorn in the stomach, heard him grunt and saw him fall back. A man leaped on Graydon, who fell forward, face smashing into the dust, the weight of the man bearing him down. He struggled to lift his head, his eyes dirt-filled and blinded.

Fingers taloned into his shoulders, and he was jerked to his feet. He could see nothing, and engulfing waves of pain made his head swim.

His head was smashed back by a fist and rocked by a second blow. A maul landed in the pit of his stomach. Fingers grabbed his hair and jerked back his head.

A voice came from a great distance, booming and fading away. A few words registered in a nightmarish manner. ". . . just a sample . . . keep on stringing wire . . . get out . . . keep your health . . ."

A fist thudded against his chin, and whirling lights exploded in one huge burst. Then there was nothing more. . . .

He became dimly aware that there was only blackness and that he was a spark of consciousness engulfed in darkness. But that passed, and he became aware of pain-clawed ribs, then legs that throbbed as he sought to move.

His eyes opened. He was lying flat, his head to one side, his eyes puffed and his face swollen. There was a taste of dirt and blood in his mouth. He moved an arm, and a spasm of pain cut like a knife.

He knew he had to get up. It was a harsh, torturing process, each muscle and nerve protesting with each slow move. But at last he stood, swaying, arms hanging, head hunched forward as he fought the agony.

Finally he looked blearily around at the blank walls of the buildings. He took a tentative step, staggered, caught himself, took another. Weaving, he moved across the yard, threaded the passage between the buildings.

He came out on the street and fell heavily against the corner of the building. The world whirled around him and he fought to keep it from spinning away.

A hand touched his arm and Graydon flinched away,

but the fingers held firm. He blinked the pain mist from his eyes and looked into Ray Decker's grim face. "You'd better come with me. You need a doctor."

Graydon had no resistance. With effort, he placed one foot before the other. Then, instead of sunshine there was shadow, and he knew he was in some kind of room.

Decker's voice came from a distance. "Stretch out on that bunk. I'll get Doc Stone."

He knew the blessed relief of lying down, and once more he slid into darkness.

He awakened to pain again, and other hands. But these were gentle, and there was the feeling of soothing ointment on his ribs and his face. He opened his eyes.

A man with a butternut face, sweeping white mustache and pouched, sad eyes smiled at him. "Well, you've come around again."

Graydon saw Decker standing over the man's shoulder. The man with the mustache looked critically at Graydon's face. "Well, that's about all I can do. Some bad bruises and cuts. No cracked ribs, but someone sure as hell tried hard. You can move any time you want to, mister, but you won't feel like it."

He stood up. Decker looked impassively at Graydon and then at the man. "Thanks, Doc."

Graydon could only look dully at the thick adobe wall above the bunk as they left. For a long time he did not move. Then he rolled painfully to one side, facing out from the wall. Then it struck him, with a shock, that he was looking at bars.

Slowly and painfully, he moved his legs off the bunk and worked himself to a sitting position. He was sitting on a narrow, hard bunk in a cell, the barred door of which was closed. He pushed himself erect, each muscle protesting.

He slowly crossed the few feet to the door, clung to the bars a moment, then lifted his voice. "Decker! . . . Decker!"

The sheriff came down the corridor and stopped before the door. "You'd better stay in the bunk a while, Graydon. Doc says it's best."

Graydon tugged at the door. "It's locked. Why?"

"I'm holding you—disturbing the peace."

"Disturbing—" Graydon stared, and then anger flushed his fever-hot face. "Me! Disturbing the peace!"

"You were fighting. I don't allow that in my town."

Graydon spoke in a choked voice, finding difficulty in forming the words with swollen lips. "I didn't start a fight. They shoved a gun in my back and beat me up. Five of them—and one was Jack Zorn."

Decker's eyes flickered. "That's your story."

Graydon exploded. "Damn it! Find out!"

"I will."

Decker started to turn away, but Graydon checked him. "Let me out."

The sheriff gave him a long, hard stare and then walked away down the corridor. Stunned and disbelieving, Graydon's hands tightened on the cold steel. He wanted to shout a curse after the lawman, but he choked it back. He crossed painfully to his bunk and eased himself down upon it.

His face felt hot, and he touched the bruises and swellings gently. Probably a pretty sight, he thought acidly. It seemed hours before he heard the distant thud of the outer door. Graydon slowly pushed himself erect. When he straightened, he saw Decker watching him through the barred cell door.

"Well?" Graydon asked.

"I've checked around town. No one saw anyone beat you up. I questioned Zorn and the rest. They know nothing about it."

Graydon took a deep breath, though it hurt his ribs. "All right, Sheriff. It's a stacked deck. I want to see Kurt Yates. He should be at the Star."

Decker shook his head. "The Arrow B crew left Tiempo hours ago."

Graydon couldn't help the angry tremble in his voice. "How much is my fine?"

Decker smiled humorlessly. "Why, there's no fine. I'm holding you in protective custody." His smile widened. "I figure by morning you'll get the idea it's bad medicine to start a fight in Tiempo."

"Morning!" Graydon exclaimed.

Decker walked away down the corridor. Anger boiled in Graydon, but he realized the futility of argument, of fuming. No matter what he said, he would stay right here. Jefferson Trent had warned Graydon how the sheriff would act. Thought of the lawyer made Graydon lift his head. He made his way to the cell door and called down the corridor to Decker.

The sheriff came and glared impatiently. "Now what?"

"I want to see Jefferson Trent."

Decker's brow rose. "Why, there's no reason to see a lawyer. You're just staying safe until I think you can go out on the street without having your teeth kicked in. It's for your own good."

He walked away, and Graydon heard the closing thud of the solid door at the end of the corridor. Graydon returned to his bunk and stretched out.

As the sun reached toward the west, the barred shadow on the floor moved slowly and climbed the far wall. Graydon tried to rest, but he was so uncomfortable he could do little more than doze. Then he heard a slight shuffle just beyond the wall. It was repeated, and he listened intently.

"Hal!" a low voice called.

He knew that voice. "Rowdy?"

"Yeah," the voice answered, a little louder now. "That damn' window's up above my head."

Graydon threw a glance at the empty corridor and, with some difficulty, stood on the bunk. He could see a can-littered back lot. Then Rowdy came into view, walking backward, peering in the window.

When he saw Graydon, his freckled face tightened. "What in hell happened to you?"

"Jack Zorn and some other peaceful citizens," Graydon answered.

"What are you doing in jail?"

"I'm being 'protected.' The sheriff doesn't like to have the peace of the town broken. How come you're in town?"

"I figured something was wrong when you didn't show up at camp. So I come in to see what happened."

Rowdy's brow knotted. "That sheriff had better learn he can't—"

Graydon cut in. "Walk easy, Rowdy."

"Hell, I'll get you out of there pronto, if I have to bring in the crew and tear the place down."

Graydon longed for just that, but caution prevailed. "Leave it alone, Rowdy. Decker would be pleased to find some excuse to throw you in jail, too."

Rowdy kicked at the dirt. "I don't like it."

"Neither do I, but we'll ride it out. Have yourself a drink or two and get back to the camp."

Rowdy argued, but finally gave in. He returned reluctantly to the main street. He stood a moment, and his eyes, moving idly along the street, caught the gilt-lettered sign of the general store. Excitement stirred in him. He crossed the street and entered. The place was crowded, and at first he did not see the girl. Then a man and a woman moved away from a counter, and he found himself looking directly into Mary Carr's soft eyes.

He pushed forward, noting the lovely pink that slowly climbed up her throat. He touched his hat. "Ma'am?"

"There are others before you," she said.

"I don't want to buy anything," he said hastily. "I wondered if I could see you home when the store closes."

She looked up at him, startled. Now Rowdy felt his own cheeks turn red. He managed a grin. "Nothing wrong in that, is there?"

"But I don't know you!"

"Sure you do! I bought a razor, remember?" He sobered. "Can't I?"

She studied him, then threw a disturbed glance at the crowd in the store. Her voice was low. "All right. Just this once. We close at nine."

His grin flashed out. "I'll meet you. I surely will!" He strode down the aisle, Mary Carr's eyes following him.

Excitement and anticipation were riding Rowdy hard when he came out on the street again. He glanced at the sky, purpling now that the sun had dipped below the horizon. He walked to the Star Saloon and pushed up to the bar. The place was busy now, crowded with riders from the big ranches. He ordered, and the busy bartender slapped bottle and glass before him. Rowdy had his drink, grinning at his reflection in the bar.

He heard Graydon's name spoken by two Association riders, who apparently felt a kinship with Arrow B. Rowdy joined them, identifying himself. He told what he knew, and their anger mounted, but Rowdy said everything would be straightened out by morning. One of the men finished his drink and hitched regretfully at his gun belt.

"Well, I've got to get back to Slash S. Wait'll the boss hears about this!"

He pushed away from the bar, went outside, mounted and headed toward Slash S. Then he drew rein and looked thoughtfully back at Tiempo's lights. With a curse, he neck-reined the horse and lined out toward the distant Arrow B.

Rowdy had another drink and then went to the town's barber. He left some time later, shaved, his hair cut and smelling of eau de cologne. He threw an impatient look at the steadily burning lights of the general store and went to the café for supper. After eating, he had no idea how many times he strolled the street, but he was at the store when Mary Carr came out.

She smiled hesitantly at him. "I really shouldn't do this."

"Why not?"

She started to answer then changed her mind. "I live just a short distance."

Rowdy fell in beside her. They passed the saddle shop as a man came out. He watched them stroll down the street, then hurried toward the Long Horn.

Mary Carr and Rowdy turned the corner and walked slowly down a dark side street.

"I met your father the other day," Rowdy said. "I thought you might be staying with him."

"I live with an aunt in town." They moved on in silence for a few moments. Suddenly she asked, "Why are you building fence?"

"It's my job."

"I know, but—it will harm so many, many people."

"They've told you that?" he asked. "That's why you don't like me?"

"But I do like—" She cut short her hasty speech. "Well, I know what they say about that fence. I know what it could do to my father."

Rowdy admitted that there would probably be a period of adjustment to barbed wire, but he tried to make her see the great, constructive change fence would eventually make. She halted before a small cottage set far back from the street, and Rowdy glanced curiously at it.

"My aunt's home," she said. "I thank you for your escort."

He fumbled desperately to hold her. "But I thought . . . It's early and—"

Her voice was gentle but firm. "I'm afraid that's impossible. I can't very well ask you in, Mr. Johnson. My aunt doesn't like fence builders."

"But I thought you understood."

"I understand how *you* feel about it," she corrected. "But we think differently here. Good night, Mr. Johnson."

"Wait!" He twisted his hat in his hands. "I won't get into town often. Maybe I could see you when I do?"

She hesitated. "I don't know."

"Talk to you in the store? Walk you home? What's wrong with that?"

She smiled at his eagerness. "Perhaps, Mr. Johnson. We'll see. I can't promise. For now, thanks and good night."

She hurried up the walk. The door opened, and he had a brief glimpse of her silhouette before it closed. Rowdy shoved his hat on his head, still looking at the house. His eyes lighted. She hadn't turned him down!

He strolled back toward the main street. His step became jauntier, and he wondered what had happened to him. No woman had ever made him look twice before, and now—

He stopped at the Star for a drink, then walked to the livery stable. Soon after, he rode by the last houses and out into the still, starlit darkness of the open range. He let the horse set a slow, ambling pace.

His loud whistle drowned the sound of hoofs as a rider came up behind him. Rowdy twisted about in the saddle, calling a friendly, "Howdy!"

"Howdy," came the reply. The rider drew abreast. His face was shadowed by the wide hat brim, but there was something vaguely familiar in the man's shape.

Rowdy peered closer. "Nice night. Heading—" He broke off short as the man cuffed his hat back and Rowdy recognized Jack Zorn. Suddenly Rowdy realized that Zorn was holding a gun on him. "Say, what is—"

"Real happy, ain't you?" Zorn asked. "Just left Mary Carr?"

"Now what business is that of yours?"

"You're trying to fence off range," Zorn said. "You're trying to fence off my girl—and you got no right to either. We'll stop it right now."

His gun exploded. The force of the slug knocked Rowdy out of the saddle. His horse shied and would have bolted, but Zorn grabbed the reins and fought it down. Zorn dismounted and ground-tied both horses. He walked back to Rowdy and looked down at him.

It had been a good day, he thought. Graydon wouldn't be worth much for a while, and now, with the superintendent gone, the fence would come to a standstill. This would also be a warning to anyone who might have ideas about Mary Carr.

Zorn looked about, caution moving under his elation. No use letting the first passer-by find Rowdy. Let them look for him come daylight. By then Zorn would be home. No chance of pinning it on him and forcing Decker's hand.

Zorn worked the slack body up over his shoulder. Some yards away, the shadowy shape of a heavy bush loomed up. He dropped Rowdy at its foot, away from the road.

He returned, picked up the dangling reins of both horses, mounted his own and headed eastward. A mile or so away, he again dismounted, removed saddle and bridle from Rowdy's horse, slapped it on the flank and watched it trot away into the darkness.

It would take its time getting home, probably stopping to graze. Satisfied, Zorn headed for his own ranch.

After a while, he started to whistle.

X

GRAYDON HARDLY TASTED THE FOOD Decker brought from the café, nor did the sheriff seem to care much. He merely glanced at the nearly untouched plate as he picked it up and left. Graydon lay on the bunk, too sore to do more than to slip off into fitful, feverish sleep, but never for long.

In a way, he was glad for the chance to rest before he made the ride to Arrow B. He was doubtful that he could stand the pounding of a horse, though by morning some of the pain should be gone. He listened to the Saturday night town noises, muffled and distant.

Graydon dozed off, only to awaken each time he moved in his sleep. Finally he slowly swung his feet to the floor and sat on the edge of the cot.

Suddenly he lifted his head, hearing a new sound, a steady drumming that grew louder, though still muffled by the thick walls. He knew that several riders had come down the street. He heard what might be voices.

There was a heavy knocking on the street door of the jail. It was repeated, then broke off. He listened, and then heard sounds just below his cell window. Graydon crouched on the floor, ready to throw himself under the bunk. There was the chance Zorn had decided to finish the job he had started this afternoon—with a bullet through the cell window.

"Graydon?"

He started, recognizing the voice. "Yates?"

"That's right. A Slash S rider told us what happened. We rode in. Irene's with us. Where's that sheriff?"

"Hal?" It was Irene. Her voice trembled with anger. "Why did they lock you up?"

Graydon pulled himself up on the bunk and called out

the window, "I disturbed the peace. I put my face in someone's fist." His voice became serious. "I'll be out in the morning. Let it go at that."

"I will not!" she called. Graydon saw her slender form in the starlight. "No one does this to any of my hands."

"I'm not one of your hands."

"You work for me. If Decker won't let you out, we'll yank out one of those barred windows."

"Irene," Graydon said urgently, "get Decker. He might listen to reason faced by your whole crew. He's the one to let me go. Don't you try a jail break. The small ranchers would like nothing better than to catch you on the wrong side of the law—in anything."

There was a silence, and then Irene spoke, the unbridled anger gone. "Kurt, take some of the boys and find the sheriff. Bring him here."

Yates looked at her, then at the black rectangle of the cell window, where he could see the white blur of Graydon's face. He had never been able to make even a suggestion and have Irene obey. But Graydon, apparently, had only to speak.

Her impatient, crisp voice startled him. "Kurt! Get the sheriff."

He named off three men, who walked with him to the street where their horses waited. Kurt noticed there were lights in the rooms over the stores, and he knew that townsmen were peering out at them. One of the men indicated another light that flashed on. "The town's waking up. Reckon there'll be trouble?"

"Tell Irene," Kurt said shortly.

He climbed into the saddle, wheeled away from the office and rode down the street, heading to the small adobe house a block away, where Decker lived.

Back at the jail, Irene came closer to the window, trying to get a clear look at Graydon's face. "What did they do to you, Hal?"

He told her briefly. She blazed at him when he finished. "And you let Decker throw you in here? And did nothing about it?"

"He practically carried me in," Graydon said dryly. "I

figured it was better to stay the night than tangle things up more by arguing about it."

A man spoke to Irene. "The town's waking up, ma'am."

"Any interference?"

"Not yet."

"See that there is none."

Graydon spoke quickly. "Irene, nothing foolish. Don't start a war here in Tiempo."

"Do I stand by and let them do as they wish?" she blazed.

"Tonight, yes."

At last Irene spoke to her rider. "I'll go out front with you." Her voice was edged with sarcasm. "There's a chance they won't shoot or beat up a woman."

Then she was gone, and Graydon slowly lowered himself to the floor. He groped his way to the cell door and strained his ears for sounds. He could hear a slight murmur, as of many voices from the street, but nothing else.

Then he heard the street door open and the heavier sound of steps in the outer office. Voices lifted, deep and angry, among them Irene's. But the closed door prevented him from hearing any words.

Then the door opened, and lamplight streamed down the corridor. Decker, Irene and Kurt Yates appeared before the door, the girl trying to see Graydon's face more clearly. Decker shifted the lamp, and Irene's gasp of dismay was loud.

She wheeled on the sheriff. "He's in that condition and you hold him here!"

"The Doc's seen him," Decker growled.

"Let him out," Irene demanded.

Decker's jaw set. "He stays. Don't threaten me with a gunfight or a jail break, ma'am. Maybe I won't win, but you won't, either."

She looked at Graydon and shock played over her face again. "What kind of law do you have in Tiempo, Sheriff? Is it fair for some and unfair for others? You're twisting it out of shape to help your friends."

Graydon came to the bars. "Irene, wait a minute. Decker, let's talk this over—alone."

"A waste of time."

"Maybe." Graydon's eyes cut to Kurt Yates and Irene. "You'll be here some time, looks like. Why not talk?"

"All right, we'll talk—but it will come to nothing."

"Irene, would you leave us?" Graydon asked. She started to shake her head, but Graydon's steady eyes gave a command. She suddenly flung about and strode back down the corridor, Kurt following.

Decker and Graydon faced each other. The sheriff spoke with hostility. "What argument you got that I haven't heard already?"

"Nothing for myself—plenty for you." Graydon grasped the bars. "How many are out in the street, watching Arrow B and working up a mad?"

"I don't know. Besides, that's my business."

"It was," Graydon said, "until Arrow B rode in. Now the town will take a hand."

"Why?"

Graydon made an impatient gesture. "Because they think Arrow B intends to break me out of here, and that you'll need help. Real trouble can start any minute, Decker. You know it. It can start by accident, touchy as everyone is."

Decker grunted. "A bluff."

"You know better. Arrow B's not bluffing. Your friends out in the street aren't. One move on either side and the whole town blows up in your face. Don't make your decision because you think someone's trying to back you down. That won't help afterwards, when you count the dead and know you caused it. You've proved to your friends you're for them. Why not let me go?"

"Let you go!"

Graydon glanced over his shoulder at the star-studded sky beyond the barred window. "It's only a few hours to daylight."

Decker frowned, wrestling with uncertainty and dislike. Then both of them heard the lifting murmur from the street. Decker suddenly walked off toward the office. Graydon's fingers tightened on the bars against the wash of disappointment and anger.

His head lifted as he heard steps and the rattle of keys.

Decker appeared, the big key ring in his hand. The lawman unlocked the door and swung it open.

"You've had your lesson," he said flatly. "Next time you cause any trouble you'll spend a month in here."

Graydon stepped out, gravely played the face-saving game. "I understand, Sheriff."

He walked stiffly into the office. Irene swung around as he entered, and Kurt, by the door, threw him a sharp, sweeping glance. Decker stalked in on Graydon's heels.

He placed the ring on the hook with a rattle of keys. "Graydon can go." He glared at Irene. "Now you and your men rattle your hocks out of town and stay out."

Her face flamed, and her chin came up. "No one orders—"

"Irene," Graydon said swiftly. "The sheriff does. This is his town. Don't argue."

He thought for a moment that her anger would be directed at him. She stood, fists clenched at the side of her dark riding skirt, eyes sparking. Then she swallowed hard. "We'll ride."

She brushed by Kurt, who stared at Graydon as he moved more slowly to the door. Graydon stood a moment on the dark porch, surrounded by Arrow B men. He saw the shadowy shapes of the saddled horses and became aware of the lights along the street, of men standing here and there on the opposite walk, beneath canopies, before doorways.

Decker pushed by him and walked out into the center of the street. He stood spread-legged, his presence telling the watchers that he still controlled the situation.

Graydon had to be assisted onto his horse. Irene leaned out of her saddle toward him. "You're all right?" she asked.

"I can ride," he said through clenched teeth, "if you don't make it a race."

The Arrow B swung out into the street. Graydon rode beside Irene, clenching his jaw against the jar of the horse.

Irene set a slow pace, as though she was even yet defying the town. But, except for the muffled thud of hoofs in the dust, there was no sound—only the sensation of hard, angry eyes upon them. The last house of the town wheeled behind them, and Graydon began to breathe easier, knowing how close a thing it had been.

Suddenly Irene made a choking sound and wheeled her horse about. She looked back at the town. The lights splashing out onto the street were distant and vague now.

"Kurt!" Her voice came like the crack of a whip.

"Right here."

"Tiempo needs a lesson."

"Irene!" Graydon pushed his horse between Kurt and the girl. "Leave well enough alone. The town doesn't need a lesson, but some others do. I'll handle that when the time comes."

"Will you?" she demanded.

"Yes."

The single word was forceful, final. Kurt covertly edged his horse toward Graydon's, trying to ease the man away from Irene. But Graydon held his mount firm. Kurt waited expectantly, slanting a look toward the distant lights.

"Let's ride," Irene said in a stifled voice.

In amazement, Kurt saw her rein her horse about. Kurt sat a moment, stunned. He wanted to shake her to make her realize that she was giving in to a stranger, a fence-builder.

He caught himself. His men milled, eying him. Kurt pushed up toward Irene and Graydon.

Then he saw that Irene's left hand was behind her, hidden from Graydon, and that she was signaling him to keep back. Kurt frowned but let them forge ahead. He saw Irene speak to Graydon, who was now riding with slumped shoulders, hands wrapped about the saddle-horn.

She dropped back until Kurt came up. She spoke in a low voice. Graydon heard the murmur, but he gave his full attention to fighting the jolting pain of his ride. It would continue for hours, he knew, and he grimly hoped that he could keep with it. Then Irene was beside him again.

He rode on, dulled. Then he slowly realized that the

sound of many hoofs had diminished. He looked around to see only Irene and one of the Arrow B hands. Kurt Yates and the rest were gone.

Graydon reined in. "Where are they?"

Irene placed her hand gently on his arm. "It's all right, Hal."

"Not back to town?"

"No. Not back to town," she assured him. He dully sensed that she was telling him the truth. He nodded and set himself again for the long journey. . . .

Shortly after dawn, Jack Zorn opened his eyes and looked up at the familiar ceiling of his bedroom. Then the events of the day before blazed in his mind. If Arrow B fence was not stopped, it certainly was badly crippled. Zorn was willing to bet Graydon'd make a wide circle around Tiempo or the small ranches, knowing that the next time would be even worse.

That red-headed superintendent wouldn't be around. The half smile froze on Zorn's thin lips, and fear touched his eyes. He shivered. Maybe there had been no need to go so far.

Zorn considered the ceiling and persuaded himself that there had been. The fence would lead to shooting anyhow, and, if this stopped it, then one dead man was better than a dozen or fifty. And there was Mary Carr. Zorn's gaunt face tightened into bitter lines.

No one tried to get his girl! But was she? a faint inner something asked. Sure! Nothing solid said between them, of course, but it was something you knew. He'd taken her to dances and church socials. It would work out if someone didn't try to worm in. That's what Johnson had done.

Zorn swung his feet out of bed. He'd best see his two riders in the bunkhouse and let them know he'd come home early from town. He grinned as he reached for his boots. Why, they could even say he was pretty drunk. Couldn't have hit a barn door at two feet even if he had pulled a gun, the condition he was in!

He stretched, feeling assured again, a strangely ludicrous figure in long wool underwear. He reached for his hat.

The bullet smashed through the window and thudded into the wall behind him. He sat petrified, hat still in his hand. Then hell broke loose. Rifles roared constantly, and bullets hit the house on every side. He heard crockery shatter in the kitchen, saw a board in the bedroom wall jump as a bullet splintered through it.

He threw himself flat on the floor as slugs smashed the remaining window panes, smacked into the walls. Over the constant thunder of guns, he heard the sounds of destruction in other parts of the house. A bullet struck the iron stove in the kitchen and screeched in an agonized ricochet.

Zorn's fingers taloned into the thin, dusty rug, and he thought of the Colt in the gun belt looped over a chair. But he dare not rise, for one of those blind but deadly slugs could find him.

Suddenly the firing ceased. Even as his ears still rang with the noise, he heard a defiant yell. Then there was the beat of hoofs and silence.

Zorn scrambled to his feet, snatched the Colt from its holster and ran at a crouch across the room to the window. He peered out and saw men, a round dozen, riding north and west. A triumphant yell came down wind. There could be no mistaking that tall figure of the man who led them—Kurt Yates. Arrow B had struck back.

Zorn began to shake. What was this attack for? A beating—or a murder?

XI

ZORN DID NOT MOVE from the window until Arrow B disappeared behind a distant, low ridge. His fingers gripped the Colt until the knuckles showed white, and his eyes sparked with dark fury. But he knew better than to throw a parting bullet after them.

His boots crunched glass as he turned. He jerked on his trousers, his glance swinging over the bullet-scarred walls.

A door slammed, and a harsh voice called, "Jack! Jack? You hit?"

He strode down a short hall into the kitchen and stopped short when he saw the destruction. There were deep white gouges in the kitchen table, shards of white crockery on the floor. The stovepipe had been knocked down, scattering soot.

Dawson, one of his hands, stood just within the outer doorway, a big man, heavy face slack. "Jack, you hit?"

"No. How about the bunkhouse?"

Klein, the other puncher, stepped into the kitchen behind Dawson. He looked around and pulled at a pendulous underlip, squinting at Zorn. "Some windows broken and a few slugs in the door. Looked like they wanted to hold me'n Dawson down while they worked on you."

Dawson asked in heavy wonderment, "Why'd they do it? Who was it?"

"It was Arrow B."

"Getting even for that fence builder!" Klein exclaimed.

Zorn nodded, more to stop their guessing than because he believed it at the moment. His eyes moved about the kitchen again, and he wondered how he had escaped the bullets. His fear disappeared under a shaking anger.

Dawson's dull countenance swung to Zorn. "What you aim to do? Can't let them get away with this."

Zorn snapped, "They'll pay. I'll figure a way." He took a deep breath. "Let's clean this up now."

He left them to the kitchen while he returned to the bedroom, where he could think out the meaning of this attack. He sat on the edge of the bed and scowled at the broken window. He became convinced that this was repayment for Graydon. Had Rowdy Johnson's body been found with a direct trail to Zorn, Arrow B would still be out there, seeking a death for a death.

Relief swept over him, to be followed immediately by the shaking anger he had known in the kitchen. He choked it down. He heard the pounding as the men replaced the stovepipe.

Zorn's eyes widened as a new thought struck him. By God! He could build this up so that it would have directly the opposite effect. He beat his fist in his palm, face lighting. Suppose he brought his neighbors to see the damage, telling them this was all they could expect from that damn Association unless they moved fast! They'd figure if Zorn had suffered this damage for their sake, then he would be the man to lead them.

He called down the hall. "Hey! Stop working out there. Tear it down like it was."

Klein appeared in the doorway. "What! Sure a slug didn't clip your head?"

"Of course not! Tear it up again."

Zorn went out in the kitchen and kicked down the pipe, scattered the crockery and smashed more to make it look better. His punchers watched him as if he had lost his mind. The kitchen looked worse than ever.

Zorn grinned. "Dawson, you and Klein rustle up breakfast before I ride into town and bring back the sheriff."

He returned to the bedroom to think out the rest of the plan. He had entered this fight at first only because he would be wiped out with the rest if the Association spreads cleared the range. Then he had come to see something else.

He needed a range war. Men would get scared and pull out, leaving their little spreads. Others would go down. How much easier could a man build up a ranch to match his dreams? Arrow B or one of the big ranches might also go down with the rest, and that would mean even richer pickings.

By a hint here, a suggestion there, a rumor somewhere else, even a little risky rustling of Arrow B beef, he had kept the pot boiling. And now he had built up anger about the fence to fever pitch.

Now, again, Irene Baird had done him a favor. He'd show the sheriff and everyone else what had been done to him. He'd have his neighbors so hopping mad and fearful that this might happen to them that they'd be willing to strike back.

Zorn paced the bedroom excitedly. Strike at Arrow B —but not direct. Hit the fence, tear it up and scatter the workers. Irene Baird would strike back, not knowing if she was attacking the real culprits or not. Then she would have not only the whole range but also the law against her.

After breakfast, Zorn saddled and, checking his Colt, nodded to his men and started toward Tiempo. For a time he rode with caution, hand never far from his holster. Then, after several miles and nothing suspicious, he rode more easily.

He wondered when Rowdy Johnson's body would be found. He admitted there might be suspicions, but certainly nothing to tie him in. Without that, Decker wouldn't move. Zorn's thoughts shifted to Mary Carr. When this was over and he was one of the big ranchers, it would be mighty easy to get her to marry him. He looked in the direction of the distant Arrow B and grinned. Might even have part of that range.

He chuckled. "You can worry about that, Miss High-and-Mighty!"

Irene had more immediate worries. Despite Graydon's stubborn insistence to keep riding, she had forced him to dismount and ease back against the trunk of a tree. It was there that Kurt Yates and his men found them.

Kurt came up to them slowly, seeing the worried way in which she was regarding the fence-builder. She looked up. "What happened?"

"We hit the place hard. There's no windows left, so you can figure what it must be like inside the house."

"Good! Mr. Zorn will be careful hereafter!"

She gave Kurt a covert signal to leave them, and he walked back to the men gathered about the horses. Irene turned to Graydon, and Kurt could see her talk to him but could not make out the words.

He had never seen Irene so worried or act so—he groped for the word—tender. That was it. A year ago, when Kurt himself had been thrown from a horse and had been laid up, she had never acted this way.

He felt anger at Graydon and at her—but mostly at Graydon. He had worked so slowly and so carefully the last few years. She had been brusque and distant when she first took over the spread after her father's death, and she had treated him as hardly more than another rider.

It was then that Kurt first had the idea of marrying her and acquiring control of Arrow B. Irene's attitude had not discouraged him. He understood that a girl in her position would not be likely to consider a hired hand as a husband. He had worked every way, every angle, to make her become more and more dependent upon him. It had been unobtrusive and slow, but he had seen her attitude change to one of friendship. Sometimes she had treated him almost as a partner.

She appreciated someone who was ready to carry out every order. He never crossed her, knowing that she always wanted her own way. He never pushed himself on her, but he had been sure love would come.

Now, watching her hover over Graydon, Kurt bitterly wondered if it had all gone for nothing. In amazement, he had watched Graydon defy the girl, give her orders, override her. Kurt could not understand.

But what could he do about it? The answer flashed into his mind with a startling shock. Destroy the fence. Do it so that Graydon would appear to be to blame. Irene would see that she was throwing money away on a hopeless project and would then be disgusted both with Graydon and the fence. Graydon would leave.

Kurt saw the whole plan in a series of flashing, mental pictures. But he recoiled, amazed that he could even think of such a treachery to Arrow B, to Irene. There would surely be some other way of getting rid of Graydon.

He walked to Irene, his glance slanting at Graydon as she looked up. "We ought to be getting on," he said gruffly.

Graydon moved, winced. "I'm ready."

Kurt turned on his heel and walked back to the men, Irene's protests to Graydon a mockery in his ears.

The remainder of the ride was without incident. At the ranch, Irene immediately took Graydon to the big house, helping him up the steps though Graydon felt he could make them himself. Kurt Yates watched them, hard-eyed. The new idea rushed into his mind again, but he pushed it away with a grimace and turned to the corrals.

Graydon would not go to his former room as Irene insisted. "But you're all bruised up!" she exclaimed.

"The more I move around, Irene, the better—though I admit it still hurts."

He sank into a chair in the big living room and sighed with relief. Irene poured him a drink. He thanked her with his eyes and downed it. She would have stayed close, but Graydon waved her away.

The remaining hours of the morning passed slowly. Now and then Graydon pulled himself from the chair and moved about the room. He had another drink, and the bite of the whisky spread like a warm glow through his body.

Irene came to announce the noon meal. He ate with increasing appetite and realized it was the first food he had taken since supper the night before. He returned to his chair, rested awhile and then walked slowly out on the porch.

He stood looking toward the pass in the hills and thinking he should be at the work camp. However, Rowdy would have things well in hand, and a rocker on the shady porch invited him. Graydon sank into it.

He was there an hour later when he saw a single rider come out of the pass and head toward the ranch. There was something familiar about him. Graydon walked to the porch rail and narrowed his eyes against the bright afternoon sunlight. He suddenly straightened despite the sharp catch of muscles.

Just then Irene came out. "Who's that?"

"Rance Bohlen, one of my foremen. There must be something wrong at the camp."

The rider reached the ranch yard and waved to Graydon, a hasty gesture that was somehow foreboding. Graydon waited with a growing feeling of pending trouble.

Bohlen dismounted at the rack and hurried to the porch, a tall, rangy man with direct blue eyes and a slightly snub nose above thin lips. He stopped at the foot of the steps, slanted a glance at Irene and then spoke worriedly to Graydon. "Looked in town for you. Heard the news and then came out here. Rowdy with you?"

"Rowdy?"

Bohlen nodded. "He never showed up at camp this morning. I finally went to Tiempo, but he wasn't there. I figured he'd come out here with you."

"But he didn't," Graydon said shortly.

"Maybe he had too large a night," Irene suggested.

"I checked the hotel," Bohlen said quickly. "Wasn't there, either." He looked at Graydon. "What could've happened?"

Graydon answered grimly, "Anything. I'm riding back with you, Rance."

"No! You can't!" Irene exclaimed.

"I have to, Irene. I know Rowdy. If he's disappeared, he's in trouble. Might be an accident. Might be— Have the boys saddle a horse, will you?"

She stifled her protest, seeing the determination and haunting fear in Graydon's eyes. "I'll do better than that, Hal. I'll send some of the boys with you."

Late in the afternoon, Graydon, with half a dozen Arrow B riders, rode into the camp. He was glad to dismount and let Rance ask around if Rowdy had returned. Rance soon reported. "He hasn't showed up. One of the men just came in from the fence line. He's not there, either."

Grayson liked this less and less. He turned to his horse, set his teeth and climbed in the saddle again. "We hunt him. He's between here and the town somewhere— or we'll find sign of him."

They rode slowly along the road, searching for some sign of the superintendent. It was a hopeless task along this well-traveled way. Graydon drew rein at the edge of town, and the men clustered about him. Bohlen asked in a dispirited voice, "What now?"

Graydon tried to slack off an aching leg muscle. His dark eyes studied the town, which now seemed withdrawn and secretive. He looked back the way they had come.

"We'll go back along the road, on either side of it— spread out. If any of you cut fresh trail, sing out."

They turned their horses, and Graydon took the flank on the left, Rance Bohlen the right. They started back, going very slowly now, each man covering a wide area.

A mile passed, a second. One of the Arrow B men skirted a big bush, and his horse suddenly shied. The rider brought the animal down and threw a quick glance at the bush. His voice lifted in a strident shout.

"Here he is!"

The riders changed direction, setting spurs and slanting into the bush. By the time Graydon rode up, the Arrow B man was out of the saddle and kneeling beside a prone figure. Graydon had a glimpse of red hair and a deathly pale skin as he jumped from the saddle.

The front of Rowdy's shirt was caked with dried blood, and at first Graydon believed him dead. The puncher who had found him said, "Still breathing, and that's all. He'll be lucky to be alive tonight."

Graydon knelt beside Rowdy, whose breathing was so light that Graydon could not see any movement in the chest. He took Rowdy's wrist, felt a wavery pulse, hardly perceptible.

Graydon stood up, looked hastily about. "Cut saplings," he snapped. "Make a stretcher with our coats."

The men moved fast as Graydon remained by Rowdy, fearing each moment that the pulse beneath his fingers would fade away. But it continued, weakly and irregularly. At last the makeshift stretcher was finished and Rowdy placed carefully in it.

In a few moments, the cavalcade rode slowly back toward town, the stretcher lariat fastened and swinging like a cradle between four of the riders. Graydon wanted to race time but knew that he did not dare if Rowdy was to live. He held his horse in, his own pain almost erased in his mounting worry about Rowdy.

Soon the town was just ahead. Graydon twisted in the saddle, speaking to the men. "Rowdy goes to the doctor—and no one stops us. If they try, use a gun."

They nodded grimly, and Graydon straightened, his hand close to his own Colt. They came into the head of the street and rode slowly down it, having to pass the main business section to reach the squat adobe house that was the doctor's office.

Up ahead, a man suddenly ran from the hotel to the sheriff's office. Graydon didn't halt the grim, slow pace. Heads appeared in windows, and the loafers on the saloon porch came slowly to their feet. Graydon almost prayed one of them would make a move.

Decker came out and stepped into the street, and Graydon heard a low growl of anger from his riders.

"I'll talk," he said in a low, warning voice.

He rode on, the procession behind him. Decker placed himself directly before Graydon, who reined in. He met Decker's cold eyes. "I'm taking this man to Doc Stone, Sheriff. I hope you try to stop me."

Decker's eyes flicked to the body on the stretcher, and his brows knitted. "What's wrong with him?"

"Bushwhacked, Sheriff, maybe dying." Graydon leaned forward in the saddle. "He was cut down on his way home. We found him two miles out. If he dies, it's murder." Graydon's voice lowered to an ominous growl. "Decker, if you don't find out who did it, we'll tear this town apart—and you with it."

XII

DECKER had been in a bad mood since before dawn. When Arrow B rode out with Hal Graydon in their midst, he had dispersed the crowd along the street. Time and again he had explained that he didn't need help, that no one had forced him to release a prisoner.

Finally, at home, he had tried to regain the sleep he had lost. But it would not come. After breakfast, however, things fell into their regular routine, and he felt that peace might again settle temporarily on the town.

Then Jack Zorn reported the destructive attack on his ranch. Decker sat behind his desk while Zorn paced back and forth, black eyes feverish and angry. He ranted about the rights of peaceful citizens while Decker listened with a mounting sense of anger and futility. So peace had returned to the town—but not to the range.

Zorn leaned over the desk. "Things like this can't go on, Ray. You've got to do something about it!"

Decker spoke wearily. "I'll look into it, Jack."

"You'll do more'n that!" Zorn snapped.

Decker's temper broke. "Everyone tells me how to be a sheriff, and I'm tired of it. Don't you start in, Jack." He took a deep breath, then spoke more reasonably. "I'll do what I can. But do me a favor. Next time you beat someone up, be sure you know what will follow."

Zorn smiled tightly. "Why, Sheriff, I was in the Long Horn—if you mean Graydon. You asked, remember?"

"And I got answers. But that ain't proof."

Zorn's gaunt face tightened. "They shot up my place. A lot of people will want to know what you'll do about it. I intend to tell them."

Decker sat quite still, holding himself in. The threat was obvious. Decker wanted to throw the man out, but this was not the course of wisdom if he wished to keep his star.

"I'll do all I can," he said, his voice flat.

Zorn smiled. "I figured you would."

He left, and Decker sat unmoving, his thoughts an angry turmoil. He should have thrown Zorn in jail along with Graydon. He sighed. If he had, that would have meant the end of his job next year when elections came up. Zorn would see to it.

Decker liked the town—after twelve years of wearing the badge, he was respected and comfortable. Without the star, what the hell could he do?

His choice was bitterly clear. He could be a good, no-favor sheriff and ride chuckline next year. Or he could play along and wear the star for as long as he wanted. In doing so, he would take orders from men like Jack Zorn. But only so far, Decker promised himself, only so far. A man had to have some pride in himself and his job. He left the office and went out for a drink.

Now Decker was facing Graydon over Rowdy's still form on the improvised stretcher.

"Who did it?" he blurted in shocked surprise. "When?"

"It was done last night some time. I'm warning you again, Decker—you'd better act pronto."

Decker stepped aside, and the cavalcade passed and turned in at Doc Stone's. The men carried the stretcher carefully inside.

Decker stalked into his office, slamming the door after him. He stood there a moment and then, in a burst of fury, jerked off his hat and slammed it on the floor.

"Of all the crazy, idjit, damn-fool things to do! If I could get my hands—"

He broke off short. This was exactly what Graydon wanted. Rowdy Johnson's shooting had obviously been an ambush, murder—something far different than open warfare—bushwhack. Murder had to be sought out and punished, and the instrument for so doing was the sheriff—Ray Decker.

He dropped heavily into his chair. The bushwhacker was bound to be someone who opposed the fence and hated Arrow B. That could be every man jack in town, every small rancher, the very people Decker wanted to appease.

He recalled something vaguely disturbing. He only half remembered it—some talk about this Rowdy Johnson making eyes at Mary Carr. Decker had dismissed it as just another bit of gossip that was always floating about. But now? He could see a remote tie-in with this ambush, so remote that he had no real reason to move on it.

Decker glanced at the yellow-faced clock on the far wall. He just might make a trip and be back in town right after supper. Might be wise if he wanted to work his way out of this split before some real evidence came up.

He walked out on the porch and looked down the street. The Arrow B horses were still standing before the doctor's office, but not one of the men was in sight. Decker made his decision, then, and walked to the livery stable to get his horse.

Just at sundown, he rode into the yard of Zorn's ranch. He saw, first, the three saddled horses at the rack and knew Zorn had company. Then he saw the shattered windows, the naked white scars of bullets in the walls of the house.

Decker tied his horse beside the others. He walked to the house and knocked on the door. There was a moment's delay, and then Jack Zorn flung it open. His black eyes widened with surprise.

He stepped back. "Come in, Sheriff! Me'n my neighbors have been talking things over—maybe something you should hear."

Decker stepped in. Ned Carr nodded to him from across the room, and Jobe Taylor bobbed his head. Sam Allen, owner of the Rafter A spread next to Zorn's, lifted his hand in greeting.

Zorn closed the door. "First, Sheriff, look around the house. You'll see what they did."

Decker couldn't very well talk to Zorn with the men present, so he complied. The place was a wreck, all right. When he came back to the front room, Zorn was speaking to the men with grim determination.

". . . and it can happen to you. I tell you, we can't sit back any more and let the Association run right over us. None of us are safe." He looked at Decker, smiling. "Now the sheriff is going to do something about it. That right?"

Decker nodded, impatient.

Zorn turned back to the others. "But I think we'd better move first before Arrow B—"

"Now hold on," Decker cut in. "Think things over first. Don't figure you can move without Arrow B or the Association striking back. Are you ready for that?" He looked challengingly at Zorn. "I hope you're talking about legal moves. There won't be any night riding or vigilante stuff?"

Zorn shrugged. "You fight fire with fire."

Decker shook his head. "You let me do the fighting, savvy?" He turned to the others. "You got a right to protect yourselves—but within the law. Right now, think out your moves. Remember—I'm on your side, but I have to uphold the law."

Zorn saw that he would only do more harm if he tried

to argue. "The sheriff's right. Let's get together in a few days and talk it over again. Spread the word."

Allen and Carr agreed. Jobe Taylor started to object, but Zorn adroitly silenced him. In ten minutes they filed out and rode away, agreeing to meet again.

Zorn was openly angry. "I sure don't appreciate what you did, Ray. I had them ready to fight for their rights."

"And start something you couldn't finish," Decker said shortly. "But I didn't come out here for that. Something's happened." He told Zorn bluntly of the finding of Rowdy Johnson and of the ultimatum Arrow B had given. He watched Zorn narrowly. The man acted surprised, but was not completely convincing. There was a touch of fright in his eyes, a hint of guilt in the way in which he moved about the room.

Zorn smiled tightly. "So they want to blame us? They can't get away with it."

"Someone said this Johnson fellow was seen with a girl."

"Oh?" There was a catch in Zorn's voice.

Decker nodded. "Might not mean anything, but someone's bound to look into it." He let the dead silence build up. "Didn't someone tell me you planned to buy some breed stock over in the next county?"

Zorn spoke slowly. "I thought of it. Put it off, though."

"I hear prices go up later on. Delay could be costly." Decker spoke as though thinking aloud. "I wonder who could've shot Rowdy Johnson?"

Zorn jerked slightly, and Decker did not miss it. He turned to the door and looked at Zorn. "Someone hated that fence enough to bushwhack him. Might die, too. Be a damned shame to arrest a friend for murder. Might blow over, though."

He walked out, not bothering to close the door. Zorn watched the lawman go to his horse, mount up and ride off. Zorn's gaunt face reflected a dozen conflicting emotions.

A few moments later, Klein looked up as Zorn opened the bunkhouse door. Dawson was stretched out on one of the bunks, half asleep.

"Something wrong?" asked Klein.

Zorn shook his head. "Take care of things, Klein. I'm leaving for Amarillo—on business."

"This time of day? Near sundown?"

Zorn frowned impatiently. "I don't know how long I'll be gone. I'll keep in touch."

He was gone. Klein blinked at the closed door, then looked around at Dawson. "Now what do you make of that?"

Dawson yawned. "Nothing—and I don't aim to. Amarillo and business, he said—that's what it is."

It was dark, and lamplight made a falsely peaceful glow along the street as Decker rode to the livery stable and turned his horse over to Leahy.

Leahy spat in the dust. "Arrow B's still in town—waiting."

"How about Johnson?" Decker asked quickly.

"Still alive. They say it's a miracle, bad as he was shot and long as he laid there before he was found."

Decker walked to the café. He ate, finding the food strangely tasteless, then went to his office. He lit the lamp and slumped wearily in the chair behind the desk, wondering if Jack Zorn had sense enough to take a ride. He looked up when steps sounded on the porch and the door opened.

Hal Graydon stepped inside. The lamplight made the bruises on his face look more livid, and there was a bleak, unforgiving set to his mouth and jaw. His voice was harsh. "What have you done about it, Sheriff?"

Decker took the chance that Graydon had spent all this time in Tiempo. "I scouted around, looking for sign."

"Find anything?"

On Decker's shrug Graydon sank into a chair, and the sheriff could see he was bone weary. Decker asked, "How's your friend?"

"Barely alive. He hasn't come out of it, and there's a chance he never will."

"Then he can't tell you who shot him?"

"No."

Decker looked at his hands, folded on the desk. "Maybe it would be best to wait to see if he can talk."

Graydon's dark eyes glittered. "Hoping he won't?" He stood up. "There'll be no waiting. I told you how it would be. I meant it then, and I mean it now."

Decker also arose. "I know how you feel, Graydon, him being your friend and all. I'll move fast as I can."

Graydon studied him, then walked out of the office and stood a moment on the dark porch. Then he walked toward the doctor's office. As he neared the general store, a woman came out. Graydon noted briefly that she was young and, so far as he could tell in the half light, pretty. He was surprised when she spoke suddenly.

"Aren't you Mr. Graydon—Mr. Johnson's friend?"

He wheeled about, taking off his hat. "I am."

She spoke with a rush. "I heard what happened. It's awful! How is he?"

Graydon, puzzled, told her. He looked sharply at her. "Did you know him?"

"Well, yes and no." She introduced herself as Mary Carr and told Graydon of her meeting with Rowdy, that he had walked her home the night he was shot. Graydon was surprised, but gave Rowdy credit for good taste.

"You saw nothing suspicious?" he asked. "Saw no one following you?"

"No. We walked home. He wanted to come to the house, but I wouldn't let him. Maybe if I had . . ." She caught herself. "Thanks for the news, Mr. Graydon. I'll pray for the best."

She walked away. Graydon watched her disappear around the next corner. His first impression was right—a charming and pretty girl. She undoubtedly had beaux in the town, or men who wanted to be. Yet Rowdy had stepped right in and—

The thought struck hard. Rowdy had walked in and someone didn't like it. So he was shot. Someone was jealous? Jealousy—added to range tensions and dislike of the fence?

Graydon walked swiftly to the Star and pushed open the batwings. Arrow B men were lined up at the bar, and looked expectantly at him as he entered. He signaled them outside.

He gave them instructions. They moved as a body

across the street and entered the Long Horn. Graydon pushed through the batwings first, his eyes sweeping the room. There were around ten men in the place.

They looked up in surprise and then in growing concern as the six men entered behind him and spread out to either side. All sound in the saloon stopped, all motion. Graydon's grim, bruised face held them. He made a slight signal, and the men behind him drew their guns. The bartender made a strangling noise, and a man at one of the tables jumped up. Instantly a gun centered on him.

Graydon's deep voice was a harsh growl. "Sit down—all of you."

The bartender started, "See here, you can't—"

"Shut up." Graydon's dark eyes glinted at each in turn. "I'm going to ask questions. Someone's going to answer them. Is that understood?"

XIII

GRAYDON GAVE THEM several tense moments to digest his meaning, then looked at them, slowly, one by one. Some met his eyes, others looked fearfully away. His question came suddenly. "Do all of you know Mary Carr?"

They nodded, surprised. Graydon allowed the ghost of a savage smile to touch his lips. "You get the idea. Who is her beau?"

The only sound was a nervous shuffling of feet.

Graydon broke the silence. "I want an answer. You stay right here until someone speaks up."

The bartender carefully moved his hands to the edge of the bar, and Graydon caught the slight movement. "Don't try for the scattergun, friend. You won't live that long."

The bartender's hands jerked forward and he placed them flat on the bar.

One of the others gained a spark of courage and

blurted, "You can't get away with this, Graydon."

"A matter of opinion. See how far you get to the door."

The man looked at the Arrow B riders, each with a gun in his hand. He eased back against the bar. Graydon waited another long, pregnant moment.

"Who is Mary Carr's beau? Or who claims to be?" He suddenly pointed at the bartender. "You!"

The man swallowed, hard. "Mister, I don't know. I never heard."

Graydon pointed at the next man, the next. Each in turn denied any knowledge, and Graydon's bruised face became steadily darker. He spoke softly. "Damn' few of you left to answer. Don't let the string run out. There are ways of getting an answer—Indian ways."

Feet shuffled nervously, and the men exchanged worried glances. Graydon's smile wasn't pleasant. "Don't try a bluff, gents. My best friend is dying."

The silence was now electric. There was a stir at one of the tables, and a man half rose. Graydon instantly swung to him. "All right. Speak out."

The man looked at his companions, then at Graydon. "Jack Zorn always figured he was top hand with Mary Carr."

"Jack Zorn! Where was he when my friend was shot?"

Another man spoke up quickly. "Right here."

That took Graydon by surprise. It didn't fit. Rowdy had pushed his attentions, one way or another, on a town girl. Soon after, he was shot. It had to stem from jealousy, and now Zorn's name had come to the fore.

Graydon realized that only that one man had spoken up. The rest looked studiously away. Graydon sensed the false note.

He pulled his gun from the holster slowly and held it poised, looking directly at the bartender. "Do you bear that out?"

The man nodded. Graydon's voice crackled. "Who was with him?"

The bartender pointed to the man who had spoken and then to another. The second man flinched away as

Graydon faced him and leveled the gun. "You were with Zorn right here? All the time?" Graydon lifted the gun muzzle. "God help you, friend, if you lie to me."

The man's eyes bugged and his face paled.

Graydon repeated softly, "You were with Zorn?" The man nodded, gulping. Graydon's voice lowered to almost a whisper. "All the time?"

"I—" The man wiped the back of his hand across his mouth and his eyes darted around the room. He blurted suddenly, "No—no, I left and then came back."

"You left?"

"Yeah, I went over to the saddle shop. I saw Mary Carr and—" His lips clamp shut.

Graydon slowly hooked his finger over the spur of the hammer and pulled it back with a click that sounded loud and deadly in the silent room. "Go on."

"I saw her and—this Johnson. They left the store. He was walking with her."

"With Jack Zorn's girl?" Graydon pushed.

"Yeah . . . yeah. I—thought Jack ought to know so I come over here and told him."

"And then Zorn left. That was the last you saw of him that night." Graydon half lifted the cocked Colt.

The man was stammering fearfully. "He left—finished his drink and left. That's the way it was."

Graydon looked at the bartender, and his voice held acid sarcasm. "So Zorn was here—but you forgot to say how long. I suppose that's the way you answered Decker."

No one replied. Graydon turned to the man who had blurted the truth. "You'll come with us."

The man turned and walked, stiff with fear, out the door, Graydon and the Arrow B men with him. The procession crossed the street toward the sheriff's office.

Graydon pushed open the door of the office. Decker looked at them in alarm.

Under Graydon's prodding, Eilly fearfully repeated the story he had told in the Long Horn. When he finished, Graydon gave him a contemptuous shove to the door. The man scuttled out.

Graydon faced Decker. "You warned me to have a

witness. You've had one—and nobody connected with Arrow B. Zorn wasn't around the time Rowdy was shot. He had the chance and he had reason, if Mary Carr's his girl. Is that enough for you?"

"It's enough," Decker said shortly. "Maybe not to arrest, but he'll have to answer some questions."

Graydon looked a little surprised. Decker smiled frostily. "I go strictly by the law."

"When are you going after Zorn?"

Decker glanced at the clock. "First thing in the morning, and that's a promise. Why don't you and some of your boys go out with me? That way, you won't have any doubt about what happens. Meet me in the morning?"

"All right. In the morning."

"Meet you at the café. We can have breakfast and head right out," Decker said, a hint of relief in his tone.

Graydon left the office, the Arrow B men following him. He walked down the street a short distance and then stopped. He called two of the men. "Keep an eye on the sheriff. If he goes anywhere but home, let me know."

Graydon went on to the doctor's office, where he learned there was no change in Rowdy's condition.

The next morning, he learned that there was still no change. The Arrow B men reported Decker had locked up and gone straight home, talking to no one. Graydon then went with his crew to the café, where Decker was waiting. After breakfast, they rode out to Jack Zorn's spread.

Klein and Dawson met them before the bunkhouse. "Well now," Klein said in answer to Decker's question, "Jack ain't here. He went to Amarillo yesterday, on business. Said he'd be there a spell. Anything I can do? Jack left me in charge."

"Sudden, wasn't it?" Graydon demanded.

Klein grinned. "Jack's been wanting to get down there for some time. I reckon he figured now was as good as any. The Boss don't tell me his plans."

Decker nodded. "Thanks. I'll be back. Tell Jack I want to see him."

He turned his horse, and Graydon followed him. He pulled alongside Decker. "Now what do you intend to do?"

Decker shrugged. "Zorn's in Amarillo, out of my jurisdiction. I have to wait until he comes back."

"I've heard a sheriff in one county can pick up a wanted man for a sheriff in another county."

Decker reined in, his square face set. "You've tangled a loop, friend. I can question Zorn about the shooting, but there's not enough for a warrant for his arrest. So I'm not writing to Amarillo to have him picked up. It's enough to ask questions but a hell of a long way from proving he did it." The sharpness left his voice. "Graydon, I'll do everything I can when Zorn comes back. You can't ask me to do more."

"Thanks," Graydon said shortly, "and you can depend upon me being around for a while."

He set spurs and rode off, fast, the Arrow B men taking after him, surprised at his sudden burst of speed.

Graydon raced for a mile or more, feeling the need to work off his futile anger. Decker was right, he knew. His authority did not extend to Amarillo. It was also true that Zorn had left the ranch many hours before Eilly had been forced to talk, nor had Decker sent word out to the ranch—at least not last night. In any case, Zorn would have been gone. But someone had warned Jack Zorn to leave—and Graydon did not believe the man had gone to Amarillo.

Finally he drew rein and the men pulled up beside him. "We'll head to the ranch," he said shortly.

At the ranch, Graydon answered the swift questions Irene fired at him. Her eyes sparked with anger and she wanted to take immediate action, ride to town.

"What can we do?" Graydon asked wryly. "Decker covered the situation."

"There must be something!" Irene exclaimed.

"If Rowdy dies, it's murder. Zorn knows that, and so does Decker. If Zorn didn't shoot Rowdy, it's mighty strange he rides off just at this time."

"Do you think he went to Amarillo?"

"I don't think so. I'll bet he's hiding out around

Tiempo to see how things go." He looked at Irene. "Think some of your men could be spared to search for sign of him?"

"I'll spare them."

"We better find him. It's not only this shooting, but the fence—and you." He saw her startled look and explained. "Zorn's in a tight spot if Rowdy dies—even if he doesn't. He'll fight us now with everything he's got, with all his friends. His own neck depends on beating us—and Zorn knows it."

XIV

JACK ZORN KNEW what was going on at Arrow B. He had not fled far, his hiding place being right in the heart of the big ranch, on Jobe Taylor's small spread. Jobe had given him asylum, cursing at Arrow B, quite willing to believe that Zorn was the victim of a plot aimed at leaving the small ranchers leaderless and helpless. Zorn bolstered this idea with his own version of the shooting.

For the first few days, Zorn hardly left the ranch house, for he knew that the hunt would be intense at first. During this time, Taylor and his single rider kept close touch with the course of events in Tiempo. They learned of the incident in the Long Horn when Ben Eilly had destroyed any chance for an easy alibi.

Taylor reported it, sputtering with anger while Zorn listened.

"Ben never did have no guts," Jobe spat, "and his jaw was always loose."

Zorn waved Jobe to the table. "Sit down and have some coffee." He filled two thick mugs and carried them to the table. "Forget Ben Eilly. That don't prove I shot Johnson because I wasn't in the Long Horn."

"They blame you!"

Zorn smiled. "My friends don't. I think that Association bunch did this themselves. If they can get us split up and on the run over this, they'll rule Tiempo complete." He hesitated a moment. "Heard how Johnson is?"

"Hanging on. Might live—might not."

Zorn spoke with assumed thoughtfulness. "I bet the Association hopes he dies—that way he can't tell the truth."

Taylor cursed again. "Be like 'em to finish the job. Decker's keeping an eye on your spread, waiting for you to show up. Not like Ray to go against us this way."

Zorn laughed. "He's not. It's his way of telling me to keep out of sight."

Taylor's pinched eyes gleamed with pleasure at the thought. Then he frowned. "But this ties us up. There's nothing now to keep 'em from building that damn' fence."

Zorn placed his mug on the table. "You're wrong, Jobe. Dead wrong. Now this is what we'll do. . . ."

Zorn, in the days that followed, did not confine himself to the house. The danger of a sudden visit from Arrow B had lessened, and Zorn allowed himself the freedom of the ranch yard with always, however, a cautious eye toward the horizon.

Jobe Taylor, though, had many visitors—never many at a time, always singly or in two's and three's—small ranchers whose fear and hatred of Arrow B was crystallized by the fence that stretched further and further each day.

Zorn told, time and again, of the unprovoked and destructive attack on his own spread, showing that this had been an attempt to drive him out so that it could be repeated on each of the others in turn.

The Johnson shooting was a result of the failure of the first attempt to drive him out. In some manner, and Zorn was never quite clear about it, the Association had ruthlessly sacrificed one of its own in order to forward its destructive plans against the small ranchers.

"Sure, I'm supposed to have done it," he said to convince listeners. "But it's just a step from blaming me to blaming the rest of you. If Johnson dies, you can look for hell to break loose."

So, gradually, Zorn welded the small ranchers into a group that he could control, men who had but one thought—find some way to break Arrow B and the Association before they themselves were destroyed. They looked more and more to Zorn for leadership.

Through his friends, Zorn knew of all that happened. Through them, he heard of a wandering chuckline rider who reported a large supply train far to the north, heading toward Tiempo.

Zorn's harsh face lighted when he heard the report. "It's fencing material—can't be anything else!" He laughed gleefully. "Suppose something happened to that train before it reached Arrow B?"

Their eyes widened. "Think it could?"

Zorn laughed again. "Let's see to it. Spread the word to everyone. We'll meet at the Squaw Creek crossing—every rancher and his riders. The teamsters will be real surprised to find they'll have helpers."

"Helpers?" Taylor asked.

"Why, sure!" Zorn chuckled. "No point in them having to take all that wire clean to the fence line."

During these days, Hal Graydon found little idle time. He put Rance Bohlen on Rowdy's job. Bohlen took hold fast and well, but there were still many problems and decisions that kept Graydon close to the work camp or riding the fence line. He kept in constant touch with Rowdy, and this meant daily rides into Tiempo. The redhead still clung to life, but that was about all that could be said.

Graydon checked with Decker and around town, but Jack Zorn still hadn't returned to his ranch. Graydon began to wonder if Zorn hadn't fled the country after all.

With several miles of fence built, Graydon moved the work camp, the first of many such moves he had planned on the job. The news pleased and excited Irene, and she came to the new camp, Kurt Yates riding beside her.

Graydon took them out to ride the line of completed fence, which now stretched for many miles west of the Tiempo road. The three of them drew rein where the fence ended at the road. Irene looked back along its gleaming length. "Hal, I'm pleased."

"Thanks. At least we got this section up with no trouble."

She frowned. "Are they still watching us?"

"They were—but fresh sign stopped about three days ago. I can't figure out why."

She laughed. "They've quit. They know nothing can stop the fence. With Zorn gone, there's no one to keep them stirred up. And in a day or two they'll learn of the new supply train coming in. A chuckline rider stopped at the ranch a few days ago. He saw it north of Squaw Creek."

"Now that *is* news!" Graydon's dark face lighted.

When Irene learned that he planned to ride to Tiempo to see about Rowdy, she decided to go along. "I want to see Jeff Trent and do some personal shopping anyhow. This is a good chance."

Yates suggested there was pressing work to be done at the ranch, but Irene dismissed his objection with brief words that made Yates' eyes cloud angrily. He looked away, but fell in with them as Graydon and Irene turned toward the town.

Irene's excitement touched Graydon and he fell in with her mood. They talked, most of the way, of inconsequential things and laughed often. Graydon felt drawn closer to her than ever before.

Unwittingly, they excluded Kurt Yates and he became more and more withdrawn. They did now notice when he slowly, deliberately, dropped back. They did not see the steely flash of his eyes as he watched them, nor the way his mouth gradually set in a straight, harsh line.

When they came in at the head of the street, Irene signaled Yates to come up. She smiled briefly, not realizing that some of the old crispness had returned to her voice. "Kurt, can you take care of the ranch order?" She hardly waited for his nod. "Then you go to the store. I'll be with Mr. Graydon. I'll meet you at the hotel for the ride back to the ranch."

She rode on with Graydon as Yates reined over to the store hitchrack. He slowly dismounted, his eyes following Irene and Graydon as they rode on to the doctor's office.

Yates tied the reins, trying to fight down the seething emotions that struggled for expression.

Graydon ushered Irene into the small waiting room of the doctor's office, knocked gently on the inner door. It was flung open, and Doc Stone, leathery face drawn and worried, looked at him blankly a moment and then with grim relief.

"Oh, Graydon—Miss Baird. I'm glad you're here."

"Rowdy?" Graydon asked in alarm.

"Bad. Complications. It's touch and go. I have to get back to him."

"Can I—" Graydon started.

Doc Stone shook his head. "Only in the way. If you'll wait here, I'll let you know."

He closed the door. Graydon sat down, worried.

Irene took the chair next to him and studied his dark, troubled face. She placed her hand on his arm. "Hal, I wish I could help."

He smiled and placed his hand on hers. "You are helping, Irene."

The minutes dragged on and on. Once they thought they heard steps approaching the office door, and they both straightened expectantly, only to slump back again when the sound faded away. Graydon bit at his lip and Irene sought for something that might take his mind off the worry.

"Will you always build fence, Hal?"

He considered it a moment and shook his head. "Not always fence. I guess I'm a rancher at heart. I'd like to run my own brand."

"Why don't you?"

He shrugged. "Might, some day. But ranching means settling down, and a lone man's never very good at that. Makes him crabbed and sour after a time. A man's got to have something more than himself—a woman—and she has to be the right one for him."

Irene studied her hands, her face bemused. She hardly knew she spoke. "Father taught me to be hard, but a girl doesn't really ever want to be that way. She wants someone she can trust and love. She wants a family."

Graydon looked at the floor. He wanted to look at Irene but feared that her mood would be broken.

She stirred. "I've looked for such a person. Never found him. I guess, because of Father, I didn't quite trust anyone. I tested them—sometimes without thinking about it. I've sometimes hated myself for doing it, but I'm glad I did."

He sensed there was more to her thoughts than she had actually worded. Graydon looked at her. Her eyes met his, large and luminous, filled with a strange wonder. They spoke to him without words, and suddenly he knew that here, before him, was the woman he had always sought.

His eyes must have spoken, for her lips parted and her voice was a whisper. "Hal?"

He stood up. His hands lifted her and gripped her elbows tightly, looking deep in her eyes. "Yes—you. I didn't know until—"

He kissed her, holding her close. This time she did not pull away. He placed his hand against the smoothness of her cheeks and marveled at the soft depth of her eyes. She clung to him, and then they broke apart.

They sat down again, his hand holding hers. At first they could speak only of the wonder of this great discovery. Gradually, however, Graydon thought of what it would mean to their future, and his headlong words stopped. He suddenly realized that he might become head of the Arrow B. The thought appalled him, because he wondered what Irene would do when she also realized this. She must have time to be satisfied in her own mind that she, not the ranch, was of paramount importance to him.

"Irene, we can't make any plans right away. There's Rowdy—and the fence has to be finished."

"But why do we have to—"

"Both can mean trouble," Graydon cut in gently, "and that can mean gunsmoke—open war or bushwhack. It's something we have to work out together. We've got to figure some way to bring peace to the Tiempo range so there's no fear and no trouble. We have to make everyone see that the fence is no harm to anyone."

"Peace in Teimpo?" she asked. "Now—with all that's

happened? They already hate me and the Association. They're afraid of the fence. How do we talk them out of that?"

"We have to," Graydon said firmly.

"What about Rowdy?"

He spoke in a low voice. "That's one of the reasons we can't plan anything—yet."

At that moment, Kurt Yates was nursing his third drink since coming into the Star. He leaned against the bar, the only customer, and stared moodily down into the amber liquid. He stirred as he heard the batwings whisper behind him and looked up into the mirror, half expecting to see Graydon.

But it was Decker, who came to the bar, nodded briefly to Yates and ordered. Yates finished his drink and ordered another, wondering why he did not feel the bite of the liquor. He watched the reflection of the sheriff in the mirror. Too bad that Decker hadn't kept Graydon in jail or run the damned fence-builder out of the country.

Then, slowly, Kurt began to think that through Decker he might have the chance to drive Graydon out himself. That would happen only if someone could permanently break up the fence. He considered it. The fence and Graydon gone, could Zorn and that bunch be held back?

Maybe—maybe not. Either way, it would work for Kurt Yates. A clear trail straight to Irene's heart and eventual ownership of Arrow B. Suppose Zorn didn't stop with the fence? No reason why Kurt couldn't stand as Arrow B's defender. Such a direct attack would make Irene turn to him. A double double-cross? It appealed to him.

Yates tossed off his drink and, when Decker happened to catch his eye in the mirror, made a slight signal toward the door. He walked through the batwings onto the porch. He glanced up the street toward the doctor's office and saw the two saddled horses still at the rack. What took them so long! he wondered savagely. Was Graydon holding Irene's hand instead of Rowdy's?

Decker came through the batwings. Yates did not

look around as the sheriff moved casually to the head of the steps and looked lazily up and down the street. Yates hesitated. Then memory of Graydon kissing Irene came to him.

"Nice day, Sheriff," he said.

Decker nodded, sensing that this was not the time to talk.

"Things have changed lately," Yates said. He couldn't help the slight tremble in his voice. "I'm tired of Arrow B ways. Anything I can do about it?"

Decker faced him now, hardly able to suppress the gleam of triumph in his eyes. Still wary, he said, "Why?"

Yates' jaw set. "Let's say there's someone I don't like—and what he's doing."

Decker looked toward the doctor's office. Irene Baird and Hal Graydon down there and Kurt Yates up here, mad as a teased rattler and trying not to show it. No mistaking it.

"I reckon you mean it," he said, and Yates nodded. "Give me a day or two."

Yates spoke fiercely. "And don't horse around! I might change my mind."

He walked off without so much as a backward glance. Decker remained on the porch, looking after him. He allowed himself the ghost of a smile.

He felt like a man who has just been dealt the fourth ace.

XV

GRAYDON WHEELED ABOUT when Doc Stone stepped into the reception room. The weary defeat showing in the man's eyes made Graydon's heart plummet like a leaden weight.

"Better come in, Graydon."

Graydon and Doc Stone crossed the inner office to the open door beyond that led to the hospital room.

Doc Stone touched his arm, put his finger to his lips and shook his head.

Graydon's eyes misted. He composed himself and then walked slowly to the other room. It was furnished with four narrow beds, a few chairs. Only one of the beds was occupied. Graydon hardly recognized the sunken, pale face as that of his friend. The once powerful hands now lay flaccid on the covers, and the body seemed to have lost half its weight. Only Rowdy's eyes had any life.

Graydon could hardly hear his whisper. "A hell of a note. You ought to fire me."

Graydon sat on the chair beside the bed. The doctor stood just within the doorway, closely watching his patient.

Graydon spoke gently. "Rance keeps the job moving—not as well as you, but it'll do until you're around again."

Rowdy's whisper was low. "I don't know, Hal. I just don't know."

Graydon placed his hand over Rowdy's. "*I* know, Rowdy; so does Doc Stone. Only one thing worries me. Who did this?"

A faint thread of surprise sounded in Rowdy's weak voice. "Ain't he talked about it? Not like Zorn."

Graydon looked over his shoulder at Doc Stone, who had taken half a step forward, shock showing through the mask of weariness. A witness, Graydon thought grimly.

"So it was Jack Zorn? How did it happen?"

"That night you were jailed. I didn't go straight back to the camp. There was a girl. I walked her home."

"Mary Carr," Graydon said. "She asked about you."

Rowdy's eyes lighted. "She did? No reason for that. I just saw her twice." He was silent again, then seemed to rouse himself. "Started to the camp. Felt good about Mary Carr. I think she likes me. Zorn came up. Said she was his girl and shot me before I knew what he was going to do."

He closed his eyes, and Graydon looked inquiringly at Doc Stone, who nodded, face tight with anger. Rowdy spoke again, a faint whisper. "Don't worry about me, Hal. I'll be back on the job—you'll see."

"I'll depend on it," Graydon said gruffly.

Rowdy's head rolled to one side, and his body collapsed. Doc Stone stepped up quickly and examined him. He spoke over his shoulder. "Nothing more now, Graydon."

"Is he—dead?"

"Coma—a deep one. I doubt if he'll come out of it. There's nothing you can do."

Graydon's voice tightened. "I think there is."

Stone spoke while he worked with Rowdy. "About Jack Zorn. Tell Ray Decker I heard it all."

Graydon looked at Rowdy's pallid, freckle-splotched face. He strode out of the room and across the office and jerked open the door of the reception room. Irene jumped to her feet and read the news in his harsh, stricken face. "Hal, I wish I . . . He's—gone?"

"Going." He told her what Rowdy had said. She listened, her hands on his a gentle comfort. She glanced at the closed office door. "Do you want to stay here?"

"I want to see Decker."

"I'll go with you," she said flatly. "Decker may not like Arrow B, but we still have some power in the country. He knows it."

In less than five minutes, Graydon stood before Decker's desk, while Irene sat in a chair just behind him. Graydon told Rowdy's story, stated that Doc Stone had heard it and would be a witness. The sheriff listened, face inscrutable.

"Rowdy is dying," Graydon finished, "and Zorn killed him."

Irene leaned forward, her lighter voice as implacable as Graydon's. "We demand that he be arrested for this."

Decker banged his palm down on the desk in anger and futility. "What in hell can I do? I can send a wire to the Amarillo sheriff asking him to pick up Zorn on a murder charge and to deliver him to me at the county line. I can't go over there personally and get him."

Graydon looked grimly at the lawman. "Are you sure Zorn's in Amarillo?"

"I'm sure of nothing, except that Zorn hasn't been seen at his ranch, in town, or anywhere else. I'll do all I can. I don't like murder any more than you do."

The two men glared at one another, and then Graydon surrendered. He turned to the door.

Irene stood up. "Sheriff, a lot depends upon catching this killer—for you."

She swept out, leaving Decker to digest the warning. Out on the street, she tried to soothe Graydon. "Maybe Zorn *is* gone, Hal. No one has seen him."

"No one has *said* they've seen him," Graydon said. He deliberately erased his frown as he turned to her. "I'm going back to Doc Stone's."

"Shall I go with you?"

"No, you can do more good at the ranch than here. I'll see you there when—it's over."

Irene looked down the street. "I was to meet Kurt at the hotel, but I don't see him on the porch."

"He's probably at the Star. I'll get him."

He bent to kiss her, and she clung to him a moment. She stepped back, whispering, "Everything will be all right again, darling. I know it!"

He pressed her arm and turned to the Star. She watched him a moment, then moved slowly to the hotel. Despite the sadness of Rowdy's impending death, she felt her heart lift and sing.

Graydon entered the Star and saw Kurt standing alone at the long bar. Kurt nodded to him. "You and the boss have been gone a long time. I decided to have another drink."

"I'm sorry." Graydon signaled the bartender to bring him a whisky. He told Kurt what had happened. Yates' lips twisted slightly, but there was no other expression. Graydon didn't notice, his mind filled with too many things.

"Irene's waiting for you now," he said. "Take her to the ranch. I have to get back to Doc Stone's."

"Sure she wants to go back with me?"

"Of course," Graydon said absently. "There's nothing she can do here."

Yates considered him, then turned and walked out. The liquor he had consumed seemed to have built a fire of hatred within him, an emotion that he knew must be concealed.

He mounted his horse at the general store and rode to the doctor's office for Irene's. He rode to the hotel and assisted Irene into the saddle. As they rode out of town, Irene turned in time to see Graydon, far down the street, hurrying to the doctor's office. She spoke in a worried voice. "Rowdy Johnson is dying."

"Now that's too bad." Kurt threw her a covert glance. "What'll this do to the fence?"

"The fence will be built," she said grimly. "They can't stop it—even with murder."

"What about Jack Zorn?"

"He'll be captured. He'll be punished," she said with sudden fierceness. "If Decker won't do it, then we will."

"Us! Why not let the sheriff handle it? Johnson wasn't one of Arrow B."

She faced him, eyes blazing. "Because he was Hal's best friend. When they struck at him, they struck at Hal—and me."

Yates' face was expressionless, but his eyes narrowed. Irene couldn't have said any more clearly what she thought about Hal Graydon.

At that moment, Decker was standing at the office window, staring out on the dusty street. He had clung to the hope that Johnson would not die—but now that was gone. Decker felt the pinch of contending forces more than ever. His mind turned this way and that, seeking an out. Then, at long last, he believed he could see a way. He debated with himself. His eyes circled the office, the familiar things, the only life that he knew. His lips pressed with determination.

He went to the Long Horn saloon, talked aimlessly with the barkeeper awhile and then said casually, "I just heard some news about the Association. It ought to get to the right ears. Someone who still keeps an eye on that fence."

The bartender looked sharply at Decker and then thought out loud that Sam Allen out at the Rafter A might be interested. Decker gravely thanked him and left.

The Rafter A was east of town, but a few miles out. Decker found Allen at work in the barn. The quid-chewing rancher was a little suspicious of the visit until Decker wondered aloud if anyone ever thought that the Arrow B foreman was tired of the Association ways and wanted to do something about it.

Allen's mouth hung open a moment, then he grinned. "Interesting news, Sheriff. Might be the boys would want to meet with Yates. Say—here?"

Decker smiled tightly. The first step had been taken, and he could only await developments. He hoped that they didn't come too fast and sudden.

That night, Doc Stone fought with death for Rowdy Johnson. Graydon remained at the office, helping as best he could. Just at dawn, the fight ended, and Doc Stone wearily stood up and placed the sheet over Rowdy's face. Graydon stood at the foot of the bed, his dark face like a stone mask.

Doc Stone spoke gruffly. "Get to the hotel and pile into bed, Graydon. You need it."

He herded Graydon through the office and reception room, and opened the outer door. Only then did the old man look at Graydon with tired, sad eyes. "I wish I could have done more."

"You did all you could. I know."

It was almost noon when Graydon emerged from the barbershop where, in the back room, he had selected Rowdy's coffin and made arrangements for the funeral.

He went to the sheriff's office, and Decker met him at the door. Graydon stopped, spoke levelly. "Rowdy died."

Decker said, with more sincerity than Graydon knew, "I'm sorry to hear it."

"Are you?" Graydon asked. "Is anyone, but me?" He stared challengingly. "Murder, Sheriff. What's to keep me from going to Amarillo after Zorn—or anywhere?"

Decker spoke patiently and reasonably. "Nothing, and I don't blame you. You might feel better if you did. But if you go after him, see the local sheriff first. Get yourself deputized. Don't end up putting the killer brand on yourself."

Graydon blinked. "Thanks."

He walked away. As he started by the general store on his way to the livery stable, he heard his name called from within. He stopped as Mary Carr came out.

"Mr. Graydon, I heard Mr. Johnson is—dead."

Her eyes shadowed at his nod. "Believe me, I'm sorry. I only met him twice and he seemed such a— He would have been nice to know."

"He was a fence-builder," Graydon said shortly.

She flushed and her eyes brimmed. "I know. He knew I held it against him." She made a hopeless little shrug. "But there's something else, Mr. Graydon. I've heard that you suspect Jack Zorn of having shot him."

"I no longer suspect. Rowdy talked before he died. Jack Zorn murdered him over—" He caught himself—"over the fence."

He touched his hat brim and swung away, continuing on to the livery stable. Mary Carr slowly moved into the store, her face stricken. She knew that Graydon had almost said the killing was over her.

She hurried to the back of the store and took her hat from a shelf. She spoke hurriedly to the proprietor. "I have to see my father, right away."

Far to the north, half a dozen small ranchers and half again as many of their riders met Jobe Taylor and Jack Zorn at the Squaw Creek ford. Taylor's rider had scouted the big train of freight wagons, still many miles away, and he reported it would reach the creek the next morning, maybe around noon.

Zorn led the cavalcade upstream to a place where they could pitch an impromptu camp without danger of being seen from the ford. He was jubilant and inclined to forget the one slight irritation. Ned Carr had refused to come, saying he preferred legal means of fighting to raiding.

A meager supper eaten, Zorn talked to the men. In the morning they would cripple, if not completely end, the fence that threatened them all, even the town. His enthusiasm fired them, and he capped it with the best news of all.

"One of their bunch is coming over to our side," he announced. "You know Kurt Yates. Well, he's sick of seeing them trying to drive us from graze that's rightly ours. Sam Allen will be talking to him. If Yates means it, you can bet I'll figure how to use him!"

The next morning, they took concealment on the low hillocks overlooking the Squaw Creek ford. They settled to wait, and the morning hours slowly passed.

Then they saw the dust cloud. Zorn watched the long line of heavy wagons approach, the big horses pulling steadily. His fingers tightened on his rifle.

The train approached the sluggish creek, and the wagon master, riding a rangy gray, rode forward to scout the ford. He cautiously rode out into the stream. Satisfied that there was no quicksand, he turned back and rode to the train. The first of the big wagons rumbled up to the creek. Zorn pushed his rifle forward and took aim.

As the wagon dipped down the slope to the water, he squeezed off the shot. A driver's hat jumped from his head at the flat crack of the rifle. Instantly, the low hummocks blossomed with rifle flame as the bullets tore into the wagons.

A horse went down. A man tumbled from a high seat, and another clutched at his shoulder. Drivers dropped reins and jumped from the wagons, fleeing the fire that centered on them. Two men fell and lay still. Within a matter of minutes, only the threshing teams remained with the wagons.

Zorn headed the rush down to the train. Knives slashed leather traces and hats whipped against broad flanks. The frightened horses, freed from the wagons, galloped off in every direction. Zorn shouted orders and brush was piled high under the wagons. Someone made a crude torch and darted from wagon to wagon, thrusting a flaming brand deep into the brush.

Zorn's voice lifted above the uproar, and the attackers raced back over the hills to their saddled horses. Some distance away, Zorn drew rein, and the men clustered about him. They looked back. Great billows of smoke lifted from the fiercely burning wagons, the brownish clouds staining the clear blue sky.

Zorn laughed and lifted his clenched fist. "There goes Arrow B and its damned fence!"

XVI

RANCE BOHLEN was checking the payroll in the office shack at the work camp, the door open. Now and then he heard a distant sound, but for the most part the camp was deserted, the men out on the fence line. Suddenly he became aware that he was not alone, and, startled, he lifted his head. Hal Graydon stood just within the doorway, dark face tight and grim.

He jumped up. "Hal! When did you get in?"

"Just now." Graydon moved to the desk. "You're permanent superintendent, Rance."

"You mean Rowdy's dead?"

Graydon nodded. "I've taken care of the funeral—in two days."

"The boys will want to go," Rance said. He frowned worriedly. "But they'll tear the town apart for what happened to Rowdy."

Graydon's eyes turned bitter. "Tiempo deserves whatever happens to it. Tell them and let them go. I'm riding on to Arrow B. I came to tell you the news." He looked down at the desk, frowning. "Think you can carry on the work alone?"

Rance looked sharply at him. "Why?"

"After Rowdy's funeral, I'll be gone, maybe for some time—first to Amarillo, and then most anywhere. Depends on how far Jack Zorn runs. You're in charge until I get back."

Bohlen started to protest, but Graydon crossed the office with his lithe, silent step and was gone.

The next morning, after breakfast, Graydon walked out to the corrals, where Kurt Yates was assigning the riders to their various jobs. Graydon waited as the men saddled up. Yates took a long time to give his orders, but finally the last man rode out and the foreman walked slowly toward Graydon. There was no real friendliness in his polite nod, and his eyes slanted quickly to the house, where Graydon had spent the night.

Yates' voice was flat. "I heard about Johnson. Too bad."

The near-careless note in his voice angered Graydon a little. But he dismissed it for more important things. "Have you run into any sign of Zorn?"

"Not a thing."

"You're sure they've looked everywhere?"

Yates shoved his hat back on his forehead, the gesture of a patient man. "They missed nothing. No one they talked to had seen Zorn, none of them cut any sign. I finally pulled them back to work. Had to, or we'd be way behind."

"Thanks, Kurt. Tell the boys to keep watching. Zorn might come back."

"Sure, I'll tell them." Yates turned away, walking toward the barn.

Graydon returned to the house and spent some time with Irene, setting up a program for the purchase and delivery of fence material for at least a month or more ahead. They were interrupted when Kurt Yates appeared in the office doorway.

"A wagon train is on its way," he said. "They sent a rider ahead."

Irene hastily arose from the desk. Graydon went with her down the hall to the porch, and Yates slowly followed. The rider arose from one of the steps when Irene came out, sweeping off a battered hat.

"Miss Baird, ma'am?" He continued as she nodded.

"The wagon master sent me ahead. He figured you'd want that wire and posts placed on the job, rather than here at the ranch."

"We do," she answered crisply.

"Then maybe you could send someone to guide us in?"

"Where's the train?" Graydon stepped forward.

The rider squinted up at the sun. "Should be pretty close to Squaw Creek."

Irene touched Graydon's arm. "Hal, why don't we go out ourselves? The ride will be good for both of us." She swung to Yates. "Kurt, would you saddle horses for us?"

She didn't wait for an answer but went back into the house. Yates grunted and walked toward the corrals. Graydon waited on the porch until Irene emerged, ready for the ride.

They both felt that, temporarily, they had escaped the shadow of Rowdy's death. There was a sense of release in the clean freedom of the range. They pushed the horses at a fast pace, and the miles rolled swiftly behind them. They knew the location of the wagon train, so there was no need to let the rider's slower pace hold them up. He gradually dropped behind.

Irene now and then threw searching glances at Graydon's grim face. The quick pace, the open range gradually lessened his tension and lifted some of the weight of his friend's death from his mind. The grooved lines around his mouth and nose softened, and there was a hint of sparkle in his dark eyes.

They finally checked their fast pace, and Irene pulled in closer to Graydon. He smiled at her. "The prescription worked, Doctor. I feel better."

"Thanks," she replied seriously. "You needed it, Hal. So did I." She was silent a moment. "Do you really think Jack Zorn is worth chasing?"

"And hanging," he answered flatly.

Suddenly he drew rein. Puzzled, she pulled in. He seemed to be listening. But she heard only the sigh of the wind out of the north.

"Something wrong?" she asked.

"I don't know. Did you hear gunfire—far off?"

"No."

"Must have been a trick of the wind." He lifted the reins, still listening.

"We're jumpy, Hal. We're bound to be." As they moved on, she said, "If you're set on going to Amarillo, you must think Zorn ran off."

"I have to figure that way. At least, I have to go see." The harshness returned to his face. "We'll finish the fence, Irene, and we'll make them all wish Rowdy was still alive. But Zorn is the one who pulled the trigger."

She sighed. "I wish—" She broke off, looking to the northern horizon. She pointed. "What's that?"

Graydon stared. Far ahead, the swept-blue expanse of sky was marred by lifting billows of smoke.

Irene said, with a catch in her voice, "That'd be about Squaw Creek."

"The supply train!" Graydon exclaimed. "It's been fired!"

"But who—"

"Get back to the ranch. Hurry! Send help up here."

He sank spurs and streaked away, leaving Irene sitting in stunned surprise. She looked at the brown tarnish against the sky and then toward Arrow B—all those miles back to the ranch. Kurt would have to round up the scattered men before they could make the ride to Squaw Creek. Her head swiveled again toward the lift of smoke. Hal could run into serious trouble up there. Her chin lifted and she sank the spurs. She would not let him ride into danger alone.

Hal pushed his horse fast, and he set his jaw grimly as he coaxed all he could from the mount. The brownish clouds grew larger, and Hal cursed every mile still ahead of him. He also cursed at Spaulding and Hanson for their delay in sending men to Arrow B. An armed escort for the wagon train would have prevented this had he enough men to assign to the job.

The smoke clouds rolled high now; Squaw Creek could not be far off. Suddenly, just ahead, he saw a man seated beside a rock, arms hanging limply over his knees, head bent in exhaustion. Hal instantly lifted his Colt from the holster.

As he drew near, the man raised his head with a

start. His eyes grew round, and he jumped to his feet.
Hal leveled the gun. "Stand hitched!"
The man shot his arms high in the air. "I ain't got a thing, mister! I'm just a teamster. Don't shoot!"
"I'm no bandit!" Hal snapped. He indicated the smoke that gave the sunlight a peculiar, sickish-yellow cast. "What happened?"
The teamster seemed to realize he was in no danger. He expelled his breath with a sighing gust of relief. "Road agents hit us at the ford. Never heard so many guns in my life."
"The train, man!"
The teamster looked blank. "I don't know. I run." He looked up at the smoke and added quite unnecessarily, "They must've fired it."
Graydon holstered the gun. "Help's coming. Round up your friends and get 'em to the train. Maybe we can save something."
"With them bandits—"
"Damn it!" Graydon blazed. "They're far away by now. Do as I say."
He spurred on. The road took a curve around some low hills that bordered the creek and dipped down to the stream itself. Then Graydon saw the destruction. On the far side of the creek, sparks, flames and smoke were billowing high in triumph as every wagon of the long train blazed.
Graydon saw the blackened spools of wire, some of it red hot, most of it already annealed in a useless mass. Then he saw the sprawled forms of two men, the big mound of a horse fallen in the traces. His dark eyes flashed, and he splashed across the creek.
Graydon dismounted and ground-tied his horse. He moved first to the fallen men, finding both of them were still alive, though seriously wounded. Behind him, several men were moving fearfully down the slopes of the hills to the stream. Graydon looked up when he heard them splash across the ford.
"What happened here?" he called.
They were still jumpy, suspicious. "Who are you?"
"I work for Arrow B. I was to build fence with—" He

glanced toward the burning wagons—"with this wire."

Reassured, the men quickly crossed the creek. Graydon remained beside one fallen man, speaking with the certainty of command. "Two of you help me here. The rest look after that other teamster. Patch them up. Help's on the way."

Graydon worked speedily and efficiently on the wounded man, ripping away the bloodstained shirt, setting a makeshift bandage over the bullet wound. Having done all he could, he stood up. Only then did he realize that more men had drifted down from concealment. He led the newcomers along the line of burning wagons, hoping to salvage something.

There was pitifully little. Graydon grimly counted up the cost of this in money to Irene and in delay to him. The shipment would have to be replaced as quickly as possible, and he hoped that Irene could stand the loss.

He turned from dour study of the last burning wagon to find Irene standing just behind him. Her face was pale as she looked around at the destruction.

"Irene! I told you to head for the ranch."

She spoke without taking her eyes from the wagons. "I thought you might run into trouble. I had to be sure."

He was both angered at the delay and pleased at her worry for him. He stepped to her side, and she looked up. "It's all gone, isn't it? How did it happen?"

"It's gone. I can bet who did it, but let's make sure."

More men had come out of hiding now, including the wagon master, who had a bullet nick on the arm. He ordered the wounded men moved into the shade of the bushes along the creek and sent teamsters out to round up as many of the big draught horses as they could find.

He was still a little shaky when he answered Graydon's questions. He graphically described the attack, indicating the brow of the low hills about the ford. Graydon listened, mouth growing tighter.

"Didn't get much chance to see any of them," the wagon master said. "It wasn't healthy to hang around and be polite."

Graydon spoke a word to Irene and went to his horse. They rode back across the creek and Graydon set his horse to the slope of the hill. He found plenty of sign—the scattered, empty shells of rifle cartridges, the churned earth. He traced the retreat of the ambushers to the place where they had mounted their horses.

His eyes followed the distinct trail southward. He sat his horse, grim and silent. Irene's voice shook with anger. "They'd dare do this to Arrow B!"

"They dared . . . and they had a leader."

"Jack Zorn!"

Graydon nodded. "It can't be anyone else."

He rode down the slope, Irene beside him, and followed the trail of the fleeing ambushers. In less than five minutes, he drew rein, having established its general direction.

Graydon told Irene shortly, "Get back to Arrow B fast. Send some men to help the teamsters, but send the rest of the crew with Kurt to cut this trail. It will lead us right to Zorn."

She touched his arm, her face showing concern. "He'll kill you if he has the chance."

"He won't get it," Graydon smiled briefly, a grim flash of his teeth. "Now get to riding."

He watched her go, heading directly for the distant Arrow B. Then he rode back to the creek. The wagon master had restored some semblance of order and had his teamsters grouped by the edge of the stream, some of them tending to the wounded men. There was a shout from the hills, and two more teamsters rode a couple of the big wagon horses toward the stream.

Graydon called the wagon master and told him that help would be on its way. The teamsters were to wait here until it arrived. Then Graydon rode back across the ford and picked up the trail of the ambushers.

Many miles to the south, Zorn drew rein and the ranchers clustered about him, still flushed and excited by their triumph. Zorn ordered them to scatter to confuse the trail.

"We won't rest for long," he promised. "Be ready to ride when I send the word—any day now."

They broke up, Zorn riding off flanked by Jobe Taylor

and his rider. Zorn rode with a mounting feeling of exultation. He could see his plans crystallize; it would not be too long before he would actually own much of the rich graze through which he was riding.

His soaring thoughts were jolted by Jobe's exclamation. "Two riders—who are they?"

Zorn saw two men approach from the south. Then Taylor grunted. "Sam Allen is one."

Zorn suddenly straightened. "And Kurt Yates! He's with us." His voice tightened. "Let me do the talking, Jobe. I want to make sure that jasper will help us."

The four men met and drew rein. Allen explained that he and Kurt had talked at some length and that Yates seemed to be all right.

But Zorn did not let down his guard. "How'd you slip away from your boss?"

"She and Hal Graydon rode north to meet a supply train," Kurt answered stiffly.

Zorn grinned. "They won't find much. We took care of it."

Kurt seemed surprised, but pleased. Suddenly Zorn threw a question as he would have fired a bullet. "How come you're going against Arrow B?"

"I don't like Graydon."

"Why?"

Kurt spoke in a rush. "Because he figures to walk in on Irene and Arrow B. I was top man until he come around."

"How do we know we can trust you?"

Kurt smiled tightly. "There's a Texas herd coming up from the south. I'll see they leave the trail and run smack into the fence."

"Then what?"

"I'll have them worked up enough over barbed wire by then that they won't leave much of that fence standing. You can depend on it."

Zorn considered, and Kurt hastened on. "Suppose Hal Graydon should stop a bullet?"

Zorn laughed and extended his hand. "You'll sure do for us, Yates."

Kurt looked at the extended hand, his face bleak. Then

he nodded, turned his horse and rode off, leaving Zorn with his hand extended into air.

Jobe Taylor grunted. "Now ain't that neighborly!"

Zorn chuckled. "Who cares? So long as he does the job."

XVII

GRAYDON HAD NO TROUBLE in following the trail. The attackers seemed to openly flaunt reprisal, daring anyone to come after them. The sheer audacity of it increased the anger that already seethed in Graydon.

He thought of Irene's worry about him going to Amarillo and he laughed aloud bitterly. Zorn was right here in the Tiempo country, and he had finally pushed his neighbors into open war. Graydon's face tightened. He was determined they would learn what range war meant.

If Zorn had never left the area, he had found refuge with a neighbor and friend. Graydon wondered who had harbored Zorn, and then he wondered if Decker had known all the time where the man was hidden. Graydon promised himself a showdown with the sheriff.

The trail suddenly broke up, a dozen smaller traces heading off in different directions. Graydon drew rein. Suppose he followed any one of the trails to the end and confronted the man or men who made it? They would claim innocence, and they would have lying witnesses. Decker would not move.

A plan began to shape in Graydon's mind—take care of the teamsters at Squaw Creek and then make a ranch-to-ranch search for Zorn—with or without the owners' permission.

The hiss of the bullet by his head and the flat crack of the rifle came simultaneously. Graydon's right hand slashed to his holster as his left jerked savagely on the reins and the spurs jabbed deep.

The horse whipped about, and then Graydon heard

the slapping report of the concealed rifle. The horse jerked spasmodically and, in the midst of stride, fell heavily. Graydon kicked free of the stirrups and threw himself from the saddle.

He struck the ground in a rolling fall, then came to a crouch. A third bullet sprayed dirt at his feet. He threw himself to one side, but he had a brief glimpse of blue smoke and flame from a distant clump of bushes.

He threw a slug at them, knowing as he did that the range was far too great for the Colt. The nearest cover was the fallen horse, so Graydon scrambled for it, throwing himself behind the dead animal just as another rifle bullet split the air above his head.

Graydon lay flat and caught his breath, his mind racing. So far there had been only one rifle, but Graydon wondered if others would be attracted by the shots.

The hidden rifleman had all the advantage. There was no concealment between the dead horse and the thick copse where the killer lurked. The man could cut Graydon down before he could cover half the space at a dead run. Nor could Graydon's bullets reach him. Graydon threw a glance over his shoulder, hoping to find some nearby bush or rock that might give him means of retreat. There was nothing.

Graydon looked back over his shoulder and realized that if the killer was smart, he could circle and, keeping well out of the range of the Colt, make this temporary shelter useless.

Graydon's senses stretched to the utmost for the first faint indication that the ambusher was on the prowl, but the silence remained unbroken.

It was a waiting game that Graydon didn't like, all the initiative being with the other side. He wondered if he dared risk a quick look over the horse's body. At that moment he heard the crack of the rifle and the thud of a slug into the carcass that protected him. A warning.

The empty minutes passed. Graydon turned about, facing the open land, sure the next attack would come from that direction. But nothing moved; there was no sound.

Graydon frowned, puzzled, though one thing was clear. He faced but one concealed rifle. Had there been more, he would have long since been caught in a cross fire. But even one man had the advantage. Why hadn't he taken it? Was the ambusher afraid to take the chance, slim as it was?

Graydon could not continue to crouch here; his deepest instincts cried out against it. He lifted his head slowly above the body of the horse. He caught a glimpse of the distant bushes and dropped instantly, expecting to hear the whistle of a bullet.

There was nothing. He frowned, crouched below the horse again. Either the ambusher was gone or had held his fire, hoping to entice Graydon from his concealment. Or he might be circling.

Graydon lifted his head again. There was no shot, and nothing stirred in the distant bushes. Graydon's gaze made a wide circuit of the area beyond the horse, seeing no sign of his attacker. His eyes narrowed as he judged the distance between himself and the bushes. Once he left his present protection, he would be wide open if the ambusher was still waiting.

Graydon's lips flattened. He gripped the Colt tightly and suddenly launched himself in an arching leap beyond the dead animal. Expecting the crash of a rifle, he raced in an erratic, crouching run. There was no challenge, no movement.

He reached the screen of bushes, burst through them, plowed to a halt. He stood alone. Beyond this one thick screen there was again open land with no place for concealment. His eyes caught the glint of sun from empty copper shells, and he saw the crushed grass where the sniper had knelt.

Graydon took a deep breath, shoved the Colt in its holster and cast further about. He found the place where the horse had waited, but his attacker was gone. Moving in a wide circle, reading sign, Graydon reconstructed what must have happened.

The unknown had been riding fairly fast, coming from the south. He had evidently seen Graydon and had instantly hidden behind the bushes. Then, as Graydon came into range, he had tried for a kill—and missed. Graydon looked toward his fallen horse. Why hadn't the man finished the job? The odds were all for him.

He walked back to his horse and considered his situation. Irene would probably be heading to Squaw Creek by now with the Arrow B crew. They would follow the trail after him, wasting no time. If he walked along his back trail, he would meet up with them a lot sooner than it would take to walk the many, many miles to Arrow B.

Graydon looked sharply around the horizon, then loosened his Colt in the holster. With a last glance at the dead horse, he started along his back trail.

Within a mile he began to experience the muscle strain of walking in high-heeled boots. At first it had seemed to be no more than a problem of adjustment of balance, and he did fairly well. Then the muscles began to pull, and the uneven ground seemed to set unexpected devilish traps that caused him to stumble.

He rested a while and then went on, wanting to reach the place where the ambushers had scattered. If he did not, the Arrow B party could easily miss him. He had no desire to be stranded out on this open range. He rested several times, begrudging each moment, but at last he reached his goal.

The Arrow B would come at least this far. He saw a cottonwood not far away and set himself to wait, leaning against the bole, glad to relieve his tired leg muscles.

Time passed slowly and he had to fight down impatience with the knowledge that it would take hours before the crew would appear. He watched northward for the first sight of them, and, while waiting, planned the search for Zorn.

They would start at Sam Allen's spread near Tiempo and fan out from there. The search would begin tomorrow— But then the dark thought came that tomorrow Rowdy would be buried. The day after, then, he thought with grim purpose. His mind turned to other things—Irene and the love that had come to him. This would change the whole pattern of his life, and he dwelled pleasantly on it for a time. Then the dreams vanished when he knew that none of this could happen until Zorn was found, the fence built.

He glanced at the sun, moving inexorably across the sky. He choked down impatience again and firmly set his mind to the new problem brought up by the destruction of the wire and posts.

Then he saw the Arrow B, heading toward him, following the trail. Irene led them, Kurt Yates at her side. Graydon walked toward them. They saw him and Irene instantly galloped to him, Kurt following. She drew rein.

"Where's your horse?" she asked, fright in her voice.

Graydon told what had happened. Irene had dismounted, and she looked closely at him as though to make sure that he had not been harmed. Yates sat quite still, ignoring the surprised and angry exclamations of the crew.

Graydon finished, and Kurt moistened his lips and leaned forward in the saddle. "Any idea who it was?"

"I didn't get a glimpse of him," Graydon said. "It could have been any stray from that bunch that hit the wagons. I'm sure of one thing, though."

"What?" Kurt asked sharply.

"The man's yellow. He had every chance to finish the job, but he backed off."

A flush touched Kurt's neck and face, and an angry glint appeared in his eyes, to disappear in a second.

Irene's eyes flashed. "Yellow or not, he'll pay for this. So will Zorn—the sooner the better." She indicated one of the men. "Tom, give Hal your horse. Double up with Curly and head for the ranch. The rest of us will follow the trail."

Graydon checked her. "Not a chance. The trail breaks up, scatters. We can waste a lot of time. I have a better idea."

Irene conceded. "You know best, Hal."

"We'll head back to the ranch. Then after the funeral . . ." Graydon's voice trailed off as he turned to the horse Tom surrendered to him.

Kurt allowed Graydon and Irene to ride ahead. He watched them, still feeling the sting of Graydon's words and yet knowing their truth. He could have finished

Graydon off, but that would have meant showing himself. He had been extremely cautious, not fearful, knowing there would be other chances. Even now, a Texas trail herd south of Tiempo was working its way northward. The next time Kurt had Graydon in his rifle sights, it would not be by chance.

Graydon led the way to the ambush scene to recover the saddle and bridle from the dead horse. Again, Irene wanted to follow the trail of the ambusher, but Graydon knew that the bushwhacker would have erased all sign within a mile or two.

Kurt eased back in the saddle with secret relief when Irene reluctantly agreed and they rode to Arrow B, where they found that the men from the burned wagon train had already arrived.

After supper, Graydon talked to Irene about the crippling effect of the wagon raid. She agreed to send a rider to Amarillo with a telegram ordering replacements. The amount of the loss sobered them, adding to the pall of tomorrow's funeral.

Even as they spoke in gloomy words, not far away Zorn and Jobe Taylor were working on a bottle of whisky as they celebrated the day's events. The lamp on the kitchen table cast a soft glow on Zorn's gaunt, excited face.

Jobe shook his head admiringly. "Just a month ago, we didn't have a chance against Arrow B. And now look what you've done!"

He ticked the items off on his fingers. "You took hold and brought us together. You took care of the damned fence-builder, Johnson. You saw what we could do with that supply train."

Zorn chuckled. "Don't forget Kurt Yates. If he can get those Texans to hit that fence, there won't be much of it left." He downed his drink. "Jobe, just a little bit more and we'll have no worries."

He leaned back. Arrow B could be broken up, and he'd see that he managed to come out with most of the range—the best, anyway. After that—Mary Carr.

Jobe reached for the bottle, froze, his arm in mid-air.

He turned his head, listening. "Riders coming. Several of them."

Zorn came to his feet. "See who it is, Jobe. I'll be in the bedroom."

He darted from the lighted kitchen into a small, pitch-black room. He groped his way to a window and lifted his Colt from the holster as he looked out into the starlit yard.

There were at least eight riders, he saw, and one looked like a woman. Light streamed out as Jobe opened the kitchen door and hailed them sharply.

Zorn heard a familiar voice. "It's me—Sam Allen. Ned Carr and some of the boys are with me. We want to talk to Jack."

Zorn took a deep breath of relief and replaced the Colt. His exultation returning, he reached the kitchen as Jobe stepped aside to admit the newcomers. Zorn could not conceal his start of surprise when Mary Carr walked in, her father and the other men behind her.

"Mary!" he exclaimed. "Sure good to see you!" He took a step toward her, but she looked at him with such a strange, hostile expression that he stopped short.

She spoke in a low, distant voice. "Hello, Jack."

He stared, dismayed, then caught himself when Sam Allen bellowed congratulations on the day's work. There was a flurry of backslaps and handshakes while Jobe rounded up chairs. When they were settled, Zorn noticed that Mary and her father were seated in a far corner—and now that peculiar expression was also on Ned's lined face.

He knew that since Ned was against raids and violence, Mary must be. But he'd bring them around to see differently. His quick action had made gains that even they could not deny. He launched into a boastful account of the destruction at Squaw Creek. Most of them had been there, but they enjoyed the recital.

He was about to tell of other plans when Mary's clear voice cut in. "You know that Rowdy Johnson died."

It caught him off balance. He nodded impatiently. "I heard. They—"

"He talked before he died," Mary cut in. "There was

a witness." Her voice became a scathing lash. "You're a back shooter and a murderer, Jack Zorn!"

A shocked silence held the room as the men stared. Zorn's mouth felt dry as he saw the beginning of doubt in their faces.

"He lied," Zorn said.

Ned Carr shook his head. "On his deathbed? I doubt it. My daughter told me, so I rode into Tiempo and talked to Doc Stone. She's telling the truth."

Zorn took a step toward him, but Carr went inexorably on. "Maybe you gents still want to throw in with Zorn. As for me, I can't trust that kind of man to lead me."

Zorn saw his control sweeping away and, with it, all his plans and dreams. His strident voice shattered the shocked silence. "What's wrong with you—all of you? Couldn't this still be some kind of trick on their part? What do you want me to do?"

Mary Carr spoke quietly. "If you're innocent, there's one sure way to prove it—to all of us. Go to Tiempo and surrender to Sheriff Decker."

In the deep silence she added, "Or I'll bring him here."

XVIII

ZORN STARED at Mary Carr, sensing the determination that lay behind her soft brown eyes and smooth beauty. The men looked at him, and his control of them depended upon the next few minutes. His brain moved like a darting rat, seeking this means or that. He spoke slowly. "I'll go to Decker. But I want a week before I do."

"Why?" Ned demanded.

Zorn flared, "To finish the job with Arrow B and the fence! Because when I go to Decker, I'll be in jail—exactly where the Association wants me. I didn't murder

Rowdy Johnson. They lie when they say that. But I did shoot him."

Mary's gasp was loud, but before she could speak, Zorn held up his hand. "I was on my way home that night. Johnson must have known I was in Tiempo, and he waited for me. We had words about—" His glance shot to Mary and she flushed. "Anyhow, we had an argument and Johnson went for his gun. I beat him to the shot."

"And a God's blessing you did!" Jobe Taylor put in.

The others looked at one another, and Zorn knew he had regained some ground, but he needed more.

He blazed at them. "What in hell bothers you! It was a fair fight. It was him or me in a gun draw. Like it's you or Arrow B over free range and that fence. What turns your craws, when you raided that supply train with me? You have to use every means at hand."

Mary Carr cut in. "If it was fair, why won't you go to the sheriff—now?"

"I promised to give myself up. I'm willing to stand trial. But Decker will have to put me in jail. Arrow B wants this to happen. They'll use every trick in the book to keep me there."

He paced, stopped and wheeled to face them. "I'm not afraid of a jury if I go to trial. I just don't want to see all we've done go for nothing while I'm stuck in jail."

He faced Ned Carr. "They'll delay trial while they hit you with everything they've got. You need me —outside and free—until the Association is whipped. Give me one week, and I'll turn myself in. I'm not afraid of justice. I'm not a killer."

Ned Carr looked uncertain, and Zorn could see new hope and enthusiasm in the way the men looked at one another.

Mary Carr stood up, but her father forced her back in the chair. "Wait a minute, girl. Maybe he's making sense."

"I know he is!" Sam Allen exclaimed. A last shred of doubt touched him. "Jack, sure it happened the way you said?"

Zorn nodded. "I said I'd give myself up. That's a promise."

Mary threw off her father's restraining hand. "I don't believe you."

"Why, Mary," Zorn said, and he didn't need to fake the angry jealousy that tinged his voice. "That fence-builder didn't turn your head, did he?"

Her mouth opened in surprise, then snapped shut. "Of all the. . . !" She saw the steady, questioning looks of the men.

"I heard," Jack said, "he'd been hanging around the the store and walked you home once."

"Ben Eilly seen you," Jobe Taylor cut in.

Mary's face was scarlet. Her eyes blazed, rejecting the suspicion in the face of each of them. "So you've made up your minds. You'll regret it. Dad, I'm going home."

She strode to the door and out. Ned looked around at his neighbors. "I best ride with her."

Zorn followed him outside. He spoke in a soft, urgent voice to Ned, and the old man turned.

"Ned, I got to know. How much did she think of Rowdy Johnson?"

Ned shook his head. "I don't rightly know. She come home from town mighty upset. So was I."

"I had to shoot first," Zorn said.

"Say you did, it still ruins your chances with Mary because of it."

He started away, but Zorn swung him around. "Ned, all I've asked is a week. But keep an eye on Mary. As upset as she is, she can tell what she knows to the wrong people. I know you wouldn't want that to happen."

"I'll see," Ned said slowly.

Early the next morning at the Arrow B, Kurt hitched a horse to the big ranch buggy and brought it to the house. Irene answered his knock almost immediately. She was dressed in black, ready for the funeral.

She saw, in surprise, that Kurt wore his usual work clothes. "Aren't you going with us?"

Kurt shook his head as Graydon came up behind

Irene. "Might be best I took that telegram for more wire to Amarillo and make sure it's sent."

Graydon smiled. "It's a good idea. Thanks, Kurt. I'll write it out for you."

He turned back down the hall. Irene started to follow, but Kurt checked her, suddenly wanting to back off from his treachery. He needed just one word of encouragement, a single faint hope. Like a desperate gambler, he cast the dice.

"I got to talk to you—about us." He blurted, "You've always kind of liked me."

"Of course!"

"I've tried to build up the ranch the way you want it. I've sort of hoped all along you'd see the sort of man I am." He stopped, dismayed by the way she was looking at him. He took the final plunge. "You know how I feel about you, Irene. I . . ." His voice trailed off, miserably.

Her smile was sweet. She put her hand on his arm and, for a moment, he thought all that he had believed about her and Graydon was wrong.

She spoke gently, but she might as well have used a knife. "Kurt, I've known. I've been pleased, as any girl would be. I know what you've done for Arrow B."

"Then. . . ?"

"No, Kurt. You're a wonderful friend, and I depend on you. I know I'll always be able to."

He looked at her, twisting his hat in his hand. His voice was low. "Because of Hal Graydon, ain't it?"

"No, I decided long before he came. I admit that I may have thought of you a bit, but I knew it wasn't right for us."

He started to turn, but her hurt voice stopped him. "Kurt! I'm sorry. But we can still be friends, can't we? Good friends?"

With an effort, he smiled. "Sure, I guess we can."

Impulsively, she came up on her toes and kissed him. "Thanks, Kurt. I think more of you now than I ever did."

Then she was gone. Kurt stood at the top of the steps, looking out toward the hills. Her kiss burned on his lips, and he savagely rubbed his hand across them. His cold eyes turned to the south where, miles away, a Texas trail herd worked northward. He'd camp with them tonight, and tomorrow . . .

Graydon came out and handed him a folded paper. "Thanks, Kurt, for taking this yourself. It's doing us all a favor."

Kurt shoved the paper in his shirt pocket. "Sure—and we all need favors, don't we?"

He walked away, and Graydon watched him a moment, not quite getting the man's meaning. Finally he turned back to the house.

When Garydon drove the buggy into Tiempo, he was immediately aware that the streets were empty. Some of the stores were closed as he passed them on the way to the simple white church just around the corner from Doc Stone's office.

The church was filled with the crew from the work camp, the hard, tough men subdued by this formal parting from a man whom they had all liked. Graydon led Irene to the front pew near the casket.

Rowdy lay there, freckled face peaceful as though in deep sleep, as the preacher droned through the service for the dead.

Not long after, Graydon followed the buckboard that carried the casket to the town graveyard. The preacher intoned the graveside service, and the casket was lowered into the ground. So Rowdy Johnson passed forever from physical sight.

Graydon and Irene turned away as the first shovels of dirt struck the wooden casket with a hollow sound. Bohlen caught up with Graydon as he helped Irene into the buggy. "Hal, what about the boys?"

"Let them have the day off."

Bohlen looked troubled. "They'll want to drink, and they're pretty mad about Rowdy."

Graydon looked toward the town, quiet, falsely peaceful. He turned to Irene. "I think the boys would like a drink to Rowdy. Do you mind?"

"I'll wait at the hotel," she answered.

He wheeled the buggy about, drove swiftly to the hotel. He helped Irene out, hitched the horse to the rack. Irene spoke to him from the porch. "Be careful, Hal."

He nodded grimly. "I will—but will the town?"

The work crew appeared at the far end of the street. Graydon realized that, except for his own men, the street was still empty. He looked sharply at the general store, the saddle and barber shops. All of them were closed.

The whole town's afraid, he thought. He felt a bitter pleasure as he waited for the men before the Long Horn. When they came up, he turned to the saloon.

"Hey!" Bohlen was puzzled. "I thought we were to stick to the Star."

"It's time for a change," Graydon answered, "and we might have a little excitement."

Bohlen slanted a glance at him but said nothing. Graydon mounted the steps to the saloon porch and stopped short. The doors were closed, and there was no sign of activity. He rattled the knob—locked tight.

The men crowded behind him, muttering, and one even suggested breaking in. Graydon shook his head and threw a glance at the sheriff's office, as devoid of life as the other buildings. He started toward the Star. The men milled a moment and then followed after him.

He strode down the deserted street to the other saloon and found the doors open. He pushed inside, the men at his heels. The saloon was empty, except for a nervous man behind the bar and Ray Decker nursing a glass at the far end of the heavy counter.

Decker nodded, no more. Graydon watched the barkeep slap glasses and bottles before the men. Decker pushed his bottle toward Graydon, stepped behind the bar and helped himself to an empty glass that he placed beside the bottle. "On me."

Graydon hestitated, then, with a shrug, poured the shot. "I'm surprised to be offered so much as a drink in this town," he said shortly, downing the drink. "Streets empty—stores closed, even the Long Horn. Can't tell the town from the graveyard."

"Closed for the funeral," Decker said.

"Don't tell me Tiempo mourns Rowdy Johnson!"

"My doing." Decker looked at the line of workers along the bar. "I know how you feel about Johnson. One wrong word and you'd tear the town apart. If there's no one to talk to, none of your men will have an excuse to start anything."

"Maybe none will be needed."

Decker shook his head. "Graydon, I'm not blind to what a man is because I don't like what he's doing. Like now—you've lost a friend. You blame the town, because you figure it backs Jack Zorn. You're both right and wrong, but that's not the point.

"Down under that mad, you're fair and honest. If there's no one to start a fight, you're not going to wreck the shop of some man who had nothing to do with the shooting." He made a motion toward the empty street. "So the town's dead—until you leave."

Graydon's dark face remained impassive. A single word would send his men on a destructive rampage. They were eager for it. He studied the square-jawed lawman, whose eyes directly met and held his own.

"We'll be leaving soon," he said. "But you'll hear from us. I know Zorn's somewhere near Tiempo. I intend to find him."

"That's my job, Graydon. You're not a deputy, and I'm not about to make you one."

"Do you think that's going to matter? Or that you can stop me?"

Graydon signaled Bohlen. He told the superintendent to let the men have a few more drinks and then take them back to the work camp. He went to the hotel. Shortly after, he rolled down the empty street, Irene in the buggy seat beside him.

He spoke grimly. "You're right about Tiempo. It looks much better dead than alive. We'll fence it in."

That afternoon at the ranch, Graydon told her of his plan to ferret out Jack Zorn. She listened with growing excitement and agreed to have a dozen armed men at the work camp early the next morning.

Graydon left the ranch soon after. He wanted to make sure that the crew had returned from Tiempo without incident and to lay out the work with Bohlen so that the new superintendent could handle the fence while he sought Jack Zorn.

He arrived at the camp late that night. The men were

back, several of them pretty drunk and all of them nursing disappointment that they had been unable to vent their anger over Rowdy on the town.

Graydon spent some time with Bohlen, revising the work schedule. At last he turned to the door. "I guess that lines it out for you, Rance, so you can handle it."

"So long as we have wire and posts, Hal, we'll build fence. You find Jack Zorn." Then, "Oh, forgot to tell you. There's a trail herd headed this way. They bedded about three miles south."

Graydon dismissed it with a shrug. "They must have strayed from the regular trail."

The crew left at the usual time the next morning, walking to the fence line. Graydon watched the men pour out of the camp.

Soon the camp was emptied, the only sound the muffled clatter from the cookshack. Graydon looked to the north, expecting the Arrow B men Irene had promised. His horse stood near by, rifle in the saddle boot. Graydon moved impatiently along the camp street, eager to get to the manhunt as soon as the riders arrived.

Soon he saw a dozen men coming at an easy trot from the direction of the Arrow B. Graydon's eyes lighted at the sight of them. He turned to his horse but stopped short as a thunder of gunfire sounded from the fence line.

The approaching riders pulled up, alarmed. Graydon vaulted into the saddle. He snatched the Colt from his holster and fired it into the air, catching the attention of the Arrow B men. He waved his arm for them to follow, set spurs and raced along the street.

He had no more than cleared the camp when he met one of the crew running toward him. Graydon swung his horse to block the man, a big Irishman, his left shoulder a mass of blood.

"Mike!" Graydon yelled. "What's happened?"

"Texas devils hit us! Riding and shooting! I've come for my gun. They'll be singing another tune in a minute!"

The Arrow B men raced behind him as Graydon set the spurs. He streaked toward the fence, his rowels raking. Now he could see the melee ahead. Shovels, clubs and Irish pluck were no match against Texas guns in the hands of the slashing riders. The work crew broke, streaming back for the camp.

Graydon saw a strand of wire whip away from a post, then a second. In a moment a whole section of fence was gone, except for the sturdy posts. Guns were still thundering, and several of his men were down.

There was a growing thunder from beyond the fence. Graydon reined in. Beyond the dust of the fight he saw a great, black mass head for the broken fence.

Cattle! Stampede! The attacking riders spurred away, leaving the workers to face the thundering avalanche of hoofs and horns that swept toward them.

Behind him, Graydon saw the Arrow B men. Above the noise, he could only point. The stampede would sweep over workers and fence, thunder on and destroy the work camp itself in the blind fear that rode the beasts, augmented by the shots and wild yells of the Texans who urged them on.

XIX

GRAYDON RACED toward the fence, paying no attention to the attackers, knowing that they could do little more damage here.

He swung around to follow the course of the stampeding herd, firing at them as he raced alongside the leader. He leaned down and fired the gun by the animal's ear. It swerved slightly but did not check its headlong run.

He was but dimly aware that the Arrow B riders were also trying to turn the leaders. The trained cow horse crowded the lead steer, and the big animal swerved again. Graydon's gun flashed until it was empty. He dared not risk a glance forward to see how near the camp was.

Then he realized that the lead animals had definitely changed direction. An Arrow B rider appeared momentarily close, and the man's gun blasted, his shrill cowboy yell splitting through the rolling thunder of hoofs. Graydon swept off his hat and, risking a tumble and sudden death at each racing step, leaned far out of the saddle and whipped it against the steer's head. More riders pressed in, and the breakneck race continued. Then, miraculously, they turned the head of the stampede almost on its tail and the animals milled, gradually slowing.

Only then did Graydon dare look up. The work camp sat intact but a stone's throw away, the dust from the milling herd drifting over it.

The herd would gradually come to an exhausted halt. It was no longer a danger. He swung away and, with a shout to the Arrow B men, headed back toward the destroyed fence. Most of them streamed after him, one or two staying with the herd to make sure it did not line out on another destructive path.

The Texas riders had bunched in a swift council of war. Now as Graydon and the Arrow B rode down on them, the scattered workers converged, the picks and shovels in their hands almost as deadly as the guns Arrow B had drawn. The Texans saw the situation at a glance. Every man threw his hands high in the air.

Graydon rode up, gun poised as though awaiting a wrong word or move. A grizzled puncher, tall and string-like, who seemed to be the Texans' leader, glanced worriedly about and shoved his hands higher in the air.

"No trouble, Mister," he said worriedly.

"No trouble!" Graydon exploded. "What else has this been?"

The Texan said nothing. Graydon sat for a long moment, fighting down anger that made him want to drag each man out of the saddle and pistol-whip him. At last he felt he could control his voice.

"You'd better talk," he said through set teeth.

The grizzled puncher nodded. "I'm Rio Cave, trail boss of the Running W herd."

"You've strayed considerable," Graydon snapped.

Cave made an abashed gesture. "I know it. Me'n the boys got fast-talked last night at the camp."

"I don't give a damn about last night. You'd better talk about this morning—and this." His arm swept toward the fence.

"That's what I'm coming to," Cave said desperately.

"This feller told us about the fence. He said we'd never get another head of beef to Wichita once it was built. He said something ought to be done about it right away and we looked like the hombres just tough enough to do it."

Graydon glared in high disgust. "And you believed him?"

Rio Cave spoke ashamedly. "Well, I reckon the rotgut he brought helped build us up pretty tall."

"Who was this man?"

Cave made a helpless gesture. "Never seen him before. But he sure talked how bad this fence was. He said no one in the country wanted it, but no one had guts enough to do anything about it. He said we could do ourselves and the country a favor with no trouble at all—just drive off the workers, cut the wire and stampede the herd through the camp. Done that quick, he said."

"And you've been on the trail long enough to be itching for trouble," Graydon added flatly.

"I reckon. Way he talked, it would be nothing. A little out of our way for a heap of fun we didn't expect, and no time lost worth mentioning."

Graydon holstered his Colt. "We'll see about that. First, what did this man look like?"

Cave scratched his head. "Tall gent—'bout like you. Yaller hair and blue eyes. Cowman, you could tell, and I'd say a rancher or foreman from the way he talked."

Graydon stared. This description was amazingly close to Kurt Yates. He slanted a glance at the Arrow B men and read the disbelief in their eyes.

One of them shook his head. "It just can't be!"

Suddenly one of the workers pointed. "There's Rance. He's been hit!"

Graydon saw the staggering figure beyond the ruined fence and galloped toward Bohlen.

Rance had almost reached the fence line when Graydon came up. One side of his face was streaked with blood. Graydon vaulted out of the saddle and ran up. Rance stopped and waved him off, even though he swayed. "I'll make it."

"But you're hit!"

"Creased." Rance touched the side of his face, looked at his blood-stained fingers and spoke fervently. "I hope a bullet never comes that close again!"

"I'll take you to the camp," Graydon said. "That needs cleaning and a bandage. Can you mount up behind me?"

Rance nodded, and then his face tightened. "Hal, you know who shot me? Kurt Yates!" Bohlen waved back toward a clump of bushes on a small knoll. "Sitting up there watching, like he directed the whole thing."

"I'm beginning to believe he did," Graydon said.

"Some reason, that Texas herd bothered me, and I went up there to make sure which way they'd be heading. No more'n got up there than I found out, all right.

"A bunch of them Texans came racing out of their camp and Yates split off from 'em, headed to the hill. Didn't see me until he was right on me. By then, they'd hit the work crew and was cutting wire. Kurt went for his gun, and I felt like my head blew up. Didn't know a thing until a few minutes ago."

Graydon, concealing his churning thoughts, remounted his horse and helped Rance to a place behind him. As he started back to the camp, he spoke over his shoulder. "Say nothing about this right now. I want to get back to Arrow B."

He rode up to the group still circling the captured Texans and dismounted, telling Bohlen to head on to the camp. Graydon looked at the fence, the coiled strands of cut wire. The herd had now stopped moving, the exhausted beef quite willing to graze, easily held by the two Arrow B men.

Rio Cave moistened his lips. "What you aim to do?"

Graydon snapped the order. "Get down—all of you."

The Texans worriedly dismounted. Graydon signaled to the Arrow B men. "Lead off their horses. There's a corral at the camp."

"Now wait a minute—" Cave began.

Graydon swung around, and the man recoiled. "You won't need those horses for a while. You tore down the fence, you'll put it back up. What you can't repair you'll pay for with heads of beef."

"We're not wire stringers!"

Graydon smiled, an unpleasant move of the lips. "Shuck your guns and get to work. My patience is rubbed thin."

Cave poised on the edge of refusal, but a glance at Graydon and the Arrow B men, guns leveled, changed his mind. He slowly unbuckled his gun belt and let it drop, giving gruff orders to his men to do likewise.

Graydon told the Arrow B men to see to it that Cave and his crew put the fence back up. Then he stepped to Cave. "You work straight through until the fence is fixed. The next time you come through, stay far away from us." He gave him a shove. "Now get to work!"

Graydon went to the camp and checked on Bohlen. The superintendent had had his wound cleaned and bandaged by the cook, and was working on a bottle of whisky. Graydon ordered Bohlen to make sure the Texans did a good job of repair, then release them and send them on their way.

"Keep the Arrow B men here," he finished, "in case there's more trouble. I'm riding to the ranch. Miss Baird should know about Yates, though I doubt if he'll show up there. I'll be back as soon as I can make it."

He wasted no time in getting to Arrow B. As he ran up the porch steps, Irene threw open the door. "Have you caught Zorn already?"

"No. Trouble at the fence." He led her back into the big main room. "Has Yates shown up here?"

"Kurt? No. Why do you ask?"

He told her what had happened and the part Yates had played. She listened, her eyes growing wider with shock and consternation. "But why would Kurt do this?"

Graydon answered, "He's jealous of me."

Irene nodded. "That's the only answer. Remember when he was waiting for you to write the telegram? I was out on the porch with him." She paced to the window and back. "He said he was in love with me and that your coming had made a difference between us. Hal, it's like he was giving me a last chance. I can see that now.

"He's wanted to marry me for a long time." She smiled wryly. "Or head up the Arrow B through marriage. It's not a nice thought, but then— I told him there was no chance, so he turned on us. Hal, what kind of person is he?"

"Insane, jealous. If he can't have you or the ranch, he'll destroy you both." Graydon kissed her. "I have to get back to the camp and Tiempo. Tell the boys what happened and have a couple of them guard the house. Yates might come back."

"But why must you go to Tiempo?"

"Yates could be there, and I want him in jail. He has gone over to the other side, and this will give them too much confidence unless we trip him up right away."

"I suppose so," she sighed.

Irene walked with him to the porch. She stopped short. "With all this happening, we've forgotten Zorn!"

"I haven't forgotten. Your boys are still at the camp. As soon as I get back from Tiempo, we'll turn this range upside down."

It was late afternoon by the time he stopped at the fence. The Texans were still working, the repair job almost finished. Bohlen said that the loss in materials would not be as high as expected. Graydon called Rio Cave. He told the trail boss to give him a bill of sale for enough beef to cover the amount of the loss. Cave's face turned turkey red.

"Be damned if I will! That beef goes to Kansas."

"You'll be jailed if you don't," Graydon said quietly, "you and your whole crew."

Rio glared and then surrendered. "I'll write it out."

Graydon remounted and rode on to Tiempo. He slowed his pace as he reached the first houses and loosened the Colt in his holster, in case Yates was waiting for him. His dark eyes moved sharply from store to saloon porch to building entryway as he headed for the sheriff's office. But he saw no sign of the renegade foreman.

He pulled into the sheriff's hitchrack, tying his horse

beside a buckboard. He gave it merely a glance and then walked to the sheriff's door and pushed it open. Ned Carr looked up from a chair beside Decker's desk. Mary Carr stood talking to the sheriff while Decker sat with troubled face.

Mary's eyes lighted when she saw Graydon. "Mr. Graydon! I'm glad you're here. I've just told the sheriff that Jack Zorn confessed before a dozen witnesses that he shot Rowdy Johnson. My father heard him."

"He claimed it was self-defense," Carr amended. "Johnson drew on him first."

Graydon strode into the room. "Then he's lying." He looked at Mary with a new excitement. "You heard him! Then he *is* in the area. I knew it!"

"At Jobe Taylor's ranch. He's been there all the time."

Graydon swung about to the desk, but Decker was already on his feet. A strange play of emotions passed over his face—anger, defeat and then a sudden determination that set his jaw. He pulled open the desk drawer and dropped a badge before Graydon.

"You're my deputy. You'll go with me."

Graydon looked from the badge to the sheriff, suspicious. "And who else?"

"Just us. Do you think I could get any townsman to help me arrest Zorn?"

"No. And for the same reason I wonder why you're filled with duty all of a sudden."

Decker flushed. "I promised I'd act when there was proof. Mary and Ned's statement ties in with what Johnson said. I know where Zorn is—now. Does that satisfy you?"

Graydon pinned on the badge. Decker turned to the gun cabinet, took out two rifles and handed one to Graydon, along with a box of shells.

Mary Carr came up. "I hope I've done the right thing. Jack said it was self-defense, that Rowdy drew first."

Graydon shook his head. "Rowdy wouldn't lie."

She nodded. "I don't think so, either. Not when he was dying. Jack asked for more time and promised to give himself up."

"Time for what?" Graydon asked sharply.

Ned pulled himself from the chair. "All along I've been against raiding and shooting," he said heavily. "Zorn never was, and I reckon the others agreed with him. He led the raid on your wagon train, boasts about it. He says Kurt Yates has swung over to—our side."

Graydon said shortly, "He persuaded a Texas trail crew to stampede their beef through our camp."

"What's this?" Decker demanded.

Graydon told him briefly, adding that he had come to Tiempo to have the sheriff arrest Yates. Ned Carr listened, lined face troubled.

"Jack plans something else," he said. "I don't know what." He indicated his daughter. "He wanted me to keep her quiet for a few more days. I agreed. Then I got to thinking that no one can depend on Zorn's promise. Whatever he plans would only be more destruction—outside the law. That's not my way of fighting. I couldn't think much of myself if I let him go on."

Graydon asked, "How are you handling this, Decker?"

The lawman flushed. "No-favor law—as it should have been." He turned to the door and glared at Graydon. "Are you riding with me, Deputy?"

The long miles to Taylor's spread seemed interminable, despite the fast pace they set. For a long time Decker and Graydon rode side by side without speaking. Then Decker gave Graydon a covert, sidelong glance.

"I reckon you don't figure me for much of a lawman," he said abruptly.

Graydon lifted his shoulders. "Do you?"

Decker rode a time in silence. "I got caught in a tight spot between Association and small ranchers. I figured I had to favor those who elected me—within reason. I managed to keep the peace, and there was no problem until you started building fence. Even then, I kept hoping things would work out."

"They did," Graydon said shortly.

"That damn' Jack Zorn!" Decker spat. "Wanted to be the big ace in the deck—shooting, raiding. They were smart enough, though, not to let me know about it. They knew I'd jail them."

"But you didn't ride herd on them."

"Who could? Besides, I figured there was a chance of things working out. I was wrong. This is the first time since I've worn a badge that I've favored anyone. It's the last time."

They came to Jobe Taylor's spread, and Decker led the way to the house. Both men rode with their hands close to their guns, and Graydon watched the windows of the ranch house sharply as they approached.

Taylor's rider came out of the bunkhouse. He lifted his hand in a careless greeting to Decker, then froze when he saw the sheriff's companion. He seemed ready to run back into the bunkhouse.

Decker's harsh voice forestalled him. "Where's Zorn?"

The man's jaw dropped. "Why, Sheriff, how would I know?"

"You know," Decker snapped. "Jobe's been hiding him." The lawman leaned out of the saddle, square face grim. "You lie to me and I'll see that you go to jail for aiding a fugitive. Now, where is he?"

The puncher looked confused and frightened. "Jack left. Him and Jobe and—" He caught himself.

"Kurt Yates?" Graydon asked.

The puncher glanced at Decker, who growled. "Answer him. He's my deputy."

"Yates rode in. Him and the boss and Jack was in the house a long time. Then they rode off."

"Where?" Decker demanded. He saw the stubborn lines around the puncher's mouth. "I've warned you. We got a lot of charges against Zorn, and murder's one of them."

The puncher looked trapped. "I heard them say something about the work camp. That's all I know."

Decker glanced at Graydon. "We'll head there."

The puncher gained courage. "Ray, folks won't take kindly to what you're doing."

Decker glared at him, then his anger changed to disgust—at the puncher or himself, Graydon couldn't tell. Decker neck-reined the horse and rode out of the yard,

Graydon beside him. Beyond the yard, Decker slanted a glance at Graydon. "What do you reckon they plan?"

"I don't know. But they've got something hatching. We'd better hurry."

They set spurs, glancing at the setting sun. They rode fast, and Graydon wondered what Yates and Zorn could be planning. After the stampede, everyone at the camp would be alert, ready for attack. Zorn wouldn't be the kind to move unless he was sure all the advantage lay with him.

Suddenly Decker pointed ahead. "Look there!"

Far ahead, billows of smoke were lifting up against the fading splendor of the evening sky. Graydon drew rein. Even as he looked, the clouds seemed to spread out along the horizon.

"Grass fire! That's what they planned!"

Decker's face was pale. "It'll sweep everything! No putting that out!"

Graydon noticed the direction of the wind and the way the smoke swept northward. Decker cursed. "It'll have burned through the camp by now, fast as that stuff moves."

"Arrow B's directly in its path!" Graydon swung his horse around. "Keep after Zorn and Yates. Irene's going to need all the help she can get."

He set the spurs.

XX

GRAYDON PUSHED THE HORSE unmercifully, and he strained ahead for the first glimpse of the Arrow B buildings. Now and then he looked toward the south, seeing the lift of smoke reaching up and covering the sky. Knowing the speed with which grass burns before a steady wind, Graydon knew that it was a dead-heat race between himself and the fire to the Arrow B.

He raked the spurs again. He cursed Kurt Yates for his treachery, then cursed Zorn. Had hatred so twisted them that they had no thought what fire would do? The flames would burn on until they were stopped by some stream too wide for the sparks to jump. Not only Arrow B, but many more spreads would be destroyed, all of them belonging to Zorn's friends.

Graydon's horse slowed, but again the rowels came into play. The animal gave another burst of speed. As the day waned, Graydon saw a faint, red glow along the horizon, the reflection of the flames against the pall of smoke. A rabbit streaked like a gray blur across his path, running in a blind panic of fear.

Finally he saw the Arrow B but, behind him, he could see the angry red glow and knew that within minutes he would be able to see the licking flames. He raced into the yard, vaulting from the saddle almost before the horse had stopped moving.

He ran to the house, jerked open the door and entered, calling Irene. There was no answer, and he realized the house was empty. He ran outside again, Lantern light flickered down by the barn and, beyond the yard toward the fire, he saw the shadowy shapes of several teams working abreast.

He heard hurrying steps and wheeled about to see Irene running up from the barn. She threw herself in his arms, clinging to him.

"Hal! I'm so scared!"

He glanced at the red horizon and, for the first time, saw the low flicker of the fire itself. "Can I help?"

She gestured toward the teams Hal had dimly seen. "Gang plows are making a firebreak around the buildings. Some of the boys are driving in the nearest beef. It's about all we can do."

They heard the yipping of the punchers and the rumble of hoofs from beyond the distant barn. Irene shook her head. "There's some of the beef. But the rest is gone. This will ruin Arrow B."

He put his arm around her and led her to the porch. The flames were in clear view now. The gang plows finished the circuit of the ranch and now there was a ring of bare, broken ground many feet across all around the buildings. The drivers headed the teams into the safety of the yard.

The fire came on with deadly speed, flaring now and then as the flames touched tree, bush or greasewood.

Irene asked, awed, "Who started this?"

"Kurt Yates and Jack Zorn."

"Maybe, Hal, but, actually, I brought this on myself. Oh, I thought I had reason to fence off and destroy my neighbors. But that was wrong. I should have found some means of compromise, some way that all of us could live together in Tiempo."

"Would they have let you?" he asked.

"I don't know. But the point is that I didn't give them the chance. That makes it my fault."

"It's a hard way to look at it."

"But the right way." She indicated the approaching flames. "It doesn't much matter anyhow. Big and little rancher will all be broke together. The fire won't leave much."

He held her close beside him and grimly watched the fire approach. The acrid smell of smoke was strong. He wondered how many head of cattle had already died in the holocaust and how many more would perish.

Irene suddenly sobbed and, half turning, buried her head on his chest. "Oh, darling, I'm so tired of trying to do a man's job and making a woman's mistakes!" She threw a tortured, defeated glance at the approaching fire. "If there's anything left, let's try to build up again—without mistakes and hate, but in peace."

He lifted her chin and kissed her.

Suddenly he realized that the fire was not advancing. He stepped to the edge of the porch, looking up to the sky, testing the breeze. The wind had changed, swinging around to the west and north. Now the flames would rage in another direction, away from Arrow B. If this northern rim could be held, then Irene would be safe.

He watched the fire closely to confirm his belief. It was coming no closer. He raced away from the house, shouting for the men, sending them out to contain the rim of fire that was burning with less ferocity here. To the east the flames raced hungrily on.

He fought with the men, beating at little tongues of flame, smothering them. Now and then there would be a small flare-up that Graydon fought savagely. At last he stood back and mopped his sweating, ash-blackened face. The danger was over. Patrolling and ordinary precautions would hold the fire.

He returned to the house and told Irene the terror had passed. The greater portion of Arrow B graze had been saved by this freakish change of the wind, but Graydon wondered what had happened to the work camp and his men. He looked off in the direction that the fire was now burning.

"Zorn and Jobe Taylor's spreads will catch it now." His voice deepened. "I guess it's a sort of justice working out."

"How about Tiempo?" Irene asked.

He judged the direction of the wind, shrugged. "Should go north of the town." He looked south. "I have to see about my crew."

She protested, but saw that he worried too much about his men. She watched him saddle a fresh horse and ride off.

The night ride was weird. The billowing smoke clouds had passed on, leaving bright starlight, the only familiar thing in a very strange world. On either side of the gray line of road extended the charcoal black of the burned prairie, relieved here and there by still burning embers.

The smell of burned grass and wood was everywhere. Now and then the breeze would pick up ash and blow it across the road in amorphous, ghostly shapes. The horse shied constantly, and Graydon had to keep a tight rein.

At last Graydon struck the work trail from the main road to the camp and turned into it. He was fearful of what he might find. He saw the winking red eyes everywhere. Only when he realized that many of them were moving did Graydon know that some were lanterns from the distant camp. He spurred the horse along the trail.

He did not recognize the ash-blackened faces as that of his own crew until a rich Irish voice called him. He dismounted, peered through the darkness and saw the welcome shadows of the camp buildings. Rance Bohlen came up.

The superintendent's eyes were two bright holes in a mask of smeared black. "Hal! Sure glad to see you!"

"Anyone hurt?" Graydon asked quickly.

"A few burns. I thought the whole camp would go, but, thank God, in the weeks we've been here we trampled out the grass. Nothing but bare ground around the buildings and corrals."

Graydon felt a flood of relief that was almost weakening. There was a ring of workers around the camp keeping a wary eye for any flare-ups that might threaten the buildings.

Rance told him what had happened. At least five or six fires had been set simultaneously south of the camp so that the wind would sweep the flames through the fence and into the buildings. Luckily, an Arrow B man had spotted the flares and called the alarm. Rance had been able to get the men along the line where grass ended and bare, packed ground made a natural firebreak. Others he had placed to watch the buildings and had sent others to make sure the fire-wild horses would not break out of the corral and stampede right into the flames.

"A couple of roofs started," Rance finished, "but the boys beat it out. The fire swept clean around us and burned north. If hell is anything like that, I sure intend to mend my ways."

The most serious burns had been suffered by the men along the grass line, who had fought the flames with sacks and shovels. Graydon suddenly remembered the Texas herd, and Rance shook his head.

"They stampeded. They're either roasted or scattered to hell and gone. Rio Cave and his bunch are crazy wild to get after them, but no horse could stand that hot ground for long."

"Was the sheriff here?"

"He tried to find out who set the fire, asking if we'd seen anyone. No one had." Rance looked sharply at Graydon. "What about Arrow B?"

"It's safe."

Bohlen nodded. "Decker said the wind had shifted.

He yelled something about Tiempo being threatened and took off."

Graydon moistened his finger and held it aloft to determine the direction of the breeze. The fire, raging miles away by now, could swing around and descend on the town, depending on wind currents.

He turned to his horse. "Keep some men here to watch the camp. Hitch up wagons and bring the rest to Tiempo as fast as you can."

"Hal, that town has done us no favors! You mean we should fight for it now?"

"Can you let those people burn?"

"No," Rance conceded.

"I'll see you and the boys in Tiempo." Graydon stepped into the saddle.

It was well beyond midnight when he rode into the town. Every house and store was alight, and people stood in silent clusters in the street, looking to the north. The sky was a wavering, reddish glow all along the horizon.

Graydon tested the wind again, but it was blowing steadily. The town was safe, but, if the wind veered, every person and building was in danger. Outside the town, men were already working feverishly, plowing a firebreak, and each quarter hour gave them that much more chance to widen it and their measure of safety.

Graydon went to the sheriff's office, but Decker was not there. Someone said he had ridden north and east, trying to warn the small ranchers. Graydon went to the Star Saloon to wait for his men.

In a couple of hours, they rattled into town in half a dozen big wagons. Graydon told them to rest near the wagons, ready for instant action should the fire swing southward.

There was constant movement along the street. Now and then some scarehead would spread the word that the fire worked toward the town, but these reports proved to be false. Just before dawn, the angry glow against the sky was far to the east, and even the most nervous of the townsmen felt that the danger had passed. As the first gray of morning touched the eastern sky, Graydon finally dropped off into an exhausted sleep.

He awakened to discover that some of the men had stretched blankets across the high sides of the wagon in which he was sleeping to form a shield against the sun. Graydon arose hastily, feeling the catch of sore muscles.

He jumped out over the tailgate. People were moving along the street, going in and out of stores, but without the normal daily rhythm. Often a man would stop and look eastward or glance toward the northern end of the street, as though he still expected disaster. Graydon saw a wagon piled high with household goods, the two weary horses in the traces standing droop-headed at a hitchrack.

Rance came up, looked at the loaded wagon. "Burned out. One of the small spreads a few miles out. They came in during the night, thankful to be alive."

Graydon nodded. "I guess we all are."

He looked at his men and gave orders that they were to eat at the town's café. "I'll pay the bill. Then give them a drink and take them back to camp. They're not needed here."

He went to the sheriff's office to wait, knowing that sooner or later Decker would return. There was still a man hunt, double now, for Jack Zorn and Kurt Yates.

There was a stir of excitement up the street, and Graydon stepped away from the porch to get a better look. A man came riding in, leading a horse across which a body was lashed.

"Found him about a mile out," the man said.

"Who is he?" someone asked.

The rider shot a look at Graydon. "You're that fence-builder, ain't you? This is someone you know."

He swung out of the saddle and walked back to the body across the lead horse. Graydon now saw the bloodstain on the dead man's back. The man lifted and turned the limp head. Graydon looked into Kurt Yates' sightless blue eyes.

The man let the head drop. "Arrow B's *segundo*. Shot in the back. What do I do with him?"

Graydon's dark face was bleak and strained. "Take him to the undertaker. Decker will want to see him."

He turned away. Yates shot in the back—a sneak killer's method. Only Jack Zorn could have done it.

Shortly after, Irene came in with three of her riders. Graydon met her and took her to the hotel porch. He made her sit down, and then he told her about Kurt Yates. She was shocked, though she listened quietly.

She sighed when Graydon finished. "I don't know what to say, Hal. Kurt did a terrible thing when he helped set that fire. But he worked for me, and I knew him too well not to feel sorry he's dead, killed in such a horrible way."

"Jack Zorn's doings," Graydon said shortly. "I wish I knew where he is."

Ray Decker rode in, slumped wearily in the saddle. He dismounted at his office. Graydon murmured a word to Irene and hurriedly crossed the street.

Decker had just poured a drink when Graydon entered, and he looked around, eyes haggard with weariness, face ash-smeared. He pulled another glass from the drawer, filled it and silently pushed it toward Graydon. He downed his own in a single gulp.

He stood a moment, waiting for the impact of the liquor. "I needed that," he said at last. "Hell run loose last night, Graydon. Still burning, but Blue River will stop it."

"How bad?"

"Who knows yet? Sam Allen, Jack Zorn, Jobe Taylor—their places are gone, maybe four, five more. God knows how many head of beef burned, and there's three men no one may ever see again." His hand shook in anger, and he placed the empty glass on the desk. "How can a man deliberately cut loose something like that! If I ever get my hands on Zorn and Yates—"

"You can have Yates now, but he's dead," Graydon said.

He told the surprised sheriff of the finding of Kurt's body. Some of the weariness left Decker's eyes. His jaw set. "Can you figure what happened?"

Graydon nodded. "I think it was Kurt's idea to set the fire and wipe me out. Zorn threw in. Then, when the fire headed straight for Zorn's place, he knew he was ruined. He blamed Yates. They probably quarreled and Zorn shot him. The point is, where's Zorn? He's killed twice now."

Decker poured another drink and studied it a moment before he downed it. "His place's gone. Jobe and Allen are wiped out, so there's no place he could hide. Yates was found about a mile out."

Graydon leaned forward. "You mean he could be right here in town?"

"People in Tiempo backed Zorn," Decker snapped. "They don't know yet what he done last night." He hitched at his gun belt. "I think we can flush him."

Graydon walked out with Decker. The sheriff drew his gun, stepped into the middle of the street and fired it in the air three times. All movement stopped, and then men converged on the lawman. Heads popped from store doorways, and more people moved to the growing crowd around the sheriff and Graydon.

Decker gave them a full account of the fire and its destructive sweep. They listened with growing shock, and Decker did not have to tell them how close the town had come to a flaming end.

"Two men started it," he said. "One's dead. I think someone here is hiding the other, believing all his lies. I want Jack Zorn. He's murdered twice. He set the fire."

There was a stunned silence. Graydon broke it. "He could do again what he did last night. If one of you knows where he is, speak up."

A townsman moved forward, his eyes round with shock. "Jack came to my place last night. I put him up."

"Why, Bender?" Graydon demanded.

"Because of you and the Arrow B. He said you were trying to get rid of him so us little folks wouldn't have a chance to fight back." Then his shoulders slumped. "But I sure didn't know he set this fire. I won't stand by any man who did that."

"He's at your place, Bender?" Decker asked.

"Still there." Bender checked the sheriff as he moved away. "Ray, he won't give up easy. That's a fact."

Decker looked around the crowd. "How many are willing to help me get the man who nearly burned you out?"

A dozen men pushed forward. Decker gave them a curt signal and walked down the street. They trailed after him, checking their guns. Graydon caught the arm of one.

"Where's Bender's house?"

"Two streets down and to the left—third house."

Graydon hurried after the impromptu posse, but he turned off before they reached the second street. Zorn would likely fight to the end since he faced two murder charges if he surrendered. Who knew how many of the posse would be shot before Zorn was killed or captured? There had to be an end to dying on the Tiempo range.

Graydon cut over another street and then cautiously edged between two houses to look at the rear of one that faced the next street. That should be Bender's. He heard the muffled sound of the posse turning the distant corner.

Graydon's dark eyes quickly took in the small shed and outhouse at the rear of Bender's place. He listened to the growing noise of the posse and then raced forward to the shelter of the shed. The rear of the house was now but a few yards away, but there was no cover.

He drew his gun and waited. He heard Decker's voice lift in a shouted command to Zorn to surrender. Graydon made a dash for the door just as a shot sounded, muffled by the building. There was an angry shout from the crowd, and guns exploded in reply.

Graydon threw himself flat against the wall beside the door. He could hear the crash of bullets, the splintering sound of breaking glass. Zorn wouldn't take much of that, he knew. In the next instant, the door was thrown open and Zorn plunged out.

Graydon stepped from the wall. "You can't make it," he said quietly.

Zorn spun around. Graydon had a brief glimpse of the gaunt face with the staring, black eyes. He saw the lips peel back as the man swung up his Colt. Graydon's wrist twisted, and the gun bucked against his hand as he fired. Zorn's gun went off at the same time, and Graydon heard the whip of the bullet by his head.

His slug caught Zorn in the chest and drove him back and down, gun falling in a glittering arc from spasmodic fingers. Zorn fell, his head bouncing as it struck the ground. His right leg pulled up, then fell slack.

Decker charged around the house, the townsmen with him. He pulled up short when he saw Zorn. Then he looked at Graydon, who shoved his Colt back in the holster.

Graydon passed his hand wearily over his face. "He didn't wait for a hang noose."

Early that evening, the townsmen filled the Long Horn. Decker, rested now, stood at the bar, still answering questions about the fire and Zorn. From Zorn's riders, in town preparing to ride chuckline, Decker had most of the story. The rest fitted in neatly, like missing pieces of a puzzle. But those who had looked to Zorn as a leader had to be told again and again before they finally realized how misplaced their faith had been.

Decker heard the batwings open. An amazed gasp caused him to swing around, his tight nerves making his hand drop to his holster.

Hal Graydon and Irene Baird stood just within the door. Graydon's dark face was lighted with a wide smile as his deep voice filled the room, breaking the stunned silence.

"Gents, the lady has something to say."

Irene gained courage. "I want to tell you that Arrow B grass can be used to feed whatever beef is left on any Tiempo spread. Send word to the little ranches to drive their beef on my graze. They are welcome."

She looked up at Graydon and took confidence from him. She faced the men again. "This is very hard for me to say. I made a mistake, but that is over. I want to live in peace with my neighbors. Will you please pass the word?"

A man at the bar asked in sharp suspicion, "What about that fence?"

Graydon stepped forward. "The fence will be completed." He held up his hands at the low murmur. "But there will be free access to all. Nor will the town be cut off by wire."

He let that sink in a moment. "Fence marks a boundary. It shortens roundups. It allows each rancher to build up his herd and breed straight and true to the beef he wants. Sooner or later, all of you will fence. We just happen to be first. But we promise you there is no threat to anyone. The swing from open range to fence will be peaceful, so far as we are concerned."

Decker came from the bar. He studied Irene a moment and then asked bluntly, "This is a different tune than Arrow B ever sang before. What happened?"

Irene smiled radiantly. "I've met someone who has changed my life. Tell them, Hal."

Graydon chuckled. "Gentlemen, late this afternoon Miss Baird and I were married."

Decker started to grin and couldn't keep it from growing wider and wider. A man rose from one of the tables and shouted, "A bride! This calls for celebrating!"

Graydon swung Irene about and they ran out, the batwings whispering behind them. The men streamed after them, halted on the porch, peering up and down the dark street, puzzled that the couple had disappeared so quickly.

Graydon and Irene emerged from the passage between the buildings at the rear of the saloon. She stopped to catch her breath. "Think they'll find us?"

"If we stay here. Decker can't be fooled for long. Hurry!"

He took a step but she swung him around. "Don't we have time for this?"

She lifted her lips. He held her close as he bent his head for her kiss.